A GROUP OF NOBLE DAMES
BY THOMAS HARDY

THAT IS TO SAY

THE FIRST COUNTESS OF WESSEX, BARBARA OF THE HOUSE OF GREBE, THE MARCHIONESS OF STONEHENGE, LADY MOTTISFONT, THE LADY ICENWAY, SQUIRE PETRICK'S LADY, ANNA, LADY BAXBY, THE LADY PENELOPE, THE DUCHESS OF HAMPTONSHIRE, AND THE HONORABLE LAURA

"...STORE OF LADIES, WHOSE BRIGHT EYES RAIN INFLUENCE."—L'ALLEGRO . . . .

ILLUSTRATED

NEW YORK
HARPER AND BROTHERS
MDCCCXCI

"SHE BEHELD THE OBJECT OF HER SEARCH SITTING ON THE HORIZONTAL BOUGH OF A CEDAR." [See page 24.]

CONTENTS.

	PAGE
THE FIRST COUNTESS OF WESSEX	1
BARBARA, OF THE HOUSE OF GREBE	69
THE MARCHIONESS OF STONEHENGE	121
LADY MOTTISFONT	144
THE LADY ICENWAY	173
SQUIRE PETRICK'S LADY	191
ANNA, LADY BAXBY	207
THE LADY PENELOPE	218
THE DUCHESS OF HAMPTONSHIRE	234
THE HONORABLE LAURA	256

DAME THE FIRST.

BY THE LOCAL HISTORIAN.

ING'S-HINTOCK COURT (said the narrator, turning over his raerao-rancla for reference)—King's-Hintock Court is, as we know, one of the most imposing of the mansions tliat overlook our beautiful Blackmoor, or Blakeraore, Vale. On the particular occasion of which I have to speak this building stood, as it had often stood before, in the perfect silence of a calm clear night, lighted only by the cold shine of the stars. The season was winter, in days long ago, the last century having run but little more than a third of its length. North, south, and west not a casement was unfastened, not a curtain undrawn; eastward, one window on the upper floor was open, and a girl of twelve or thirteen was leaning over the sill. That she had not taken up the position for purposes of observation was apparent at a glance, for she kept her eyes covered with her hands.

The room occupied by the girl was an inner one of a suite, to be reached only by passing through a large bedchamber adjoining. From this apartment voices in altercation were audible, everything else in the building being so still. It was to avoid listening to these voices that the girl had left her little cot, thrown a cloak round her head and shoulders, and stretched into the night air.

But she could not escape the conversation, try as she would. The words reached her in all their painfulness, one sentence in masculine tones, those of her father, being repeated many times.

" I tell 'ee there shall be no such betrothal! I tell 'ee there sha'n't. A child like her !"

She knew the subject of dispute to be herself. A cool feminine voice, her mother's, replied:

"Have done with you, and be wise. He is willing to wait a good five or six years before the marriage takes place, and there's not a man in the county to compare with him."

" It shall not be. He is over thirty. It is wickedness."

" He is just thirty, and the best and finest man alive—a perfect match for her."

" He is poor."

"But his father and elder brothers are made much of at Court—none so constantly at the palace as they; and with her fortune, who knows ? He may be able to get a barony."

" I believe you are in love with en yourself!"

" How can you insult me so, Thomas! And is it not monstrous for you to talk of my wickedness when you have a like scheme in your own head ? You know you have. Some bumpkin of your own choosing—some petty gentleman who lives down at that outlandish place of yours. Falls -Park—one of your pot-companions' sons—"

There was an outburst of imprecation on the part of her husband in lieu of further argument. As soon as he could utter a connected sentence he said: " You crow and you domineer, mistress, because you are heiress-general here. You are in your own house ; you are on your own land. But let me tell 'ee that if I did come here to you instead of taking you to me, it was done at the dictates of convenience merely. H—, I'm no beggar ! Ha'n't I a place of my own ? Ha'n't I an avenue as long as thine? Ha'n't I beeches that will more than match thy oaks ? I should have lived in my own quiet house and land, contented, if you had not called me off with your

airs and graces. Faith, I'll go back there; I'll not stay with thee longer ! If it had not been for our Betty I should have gone long ago !"

After this there were no more words ; but presently, hearing the sound of a door opening and shutting below, the girl again looked from the window. Footsteps crunched on the gravel-walk, and a shape in a drab great-coat, easily distinguishable as her father, withdrew from the house. He moved to the left, and she watched him diminish down the long east front till he had turned the corner and vanished. He must have gone round to the stables.

She closed the window and shrank into bed, where she cried herself to sleep. This child, their only one, Betty, beloved ambitiously by her mother, and with uncalculating passionateness by her father, was frequently made wretched by such episodes as this; though she was too young to care very deeply, for her own sake, whether her mother betrothed her to the gentleman discussed or not.

The Squire had often gone out of the house in this manner, declaring that he would never return, but he had always reappeared in the morning. The present occasion, however, was different in the issue; next day she was told that her father had ridden to his estate at Falls -Park early in the morning on business with his agent, and might not come back for some days.

Falls -Park was over twenty miles from King's-Hintock Court, and was altogether a more modest centre-piece to a more modest possession than the latter. But as Squire Dornell came in view of it that February morning, he thought that he had been a fool ever to leave it, though it was for the sake of the greatest heiress in Wessex. Its classic front, of the period of the second

Charles, derived fi'om its regular features a dignity which the great, battlemented, heterogeneous mansion of his wife could not eclipse. Altogether he was sick at heart, and the gloom which the densely-timbered park threw over the scene did not tend to remove the depression of this rubicund man of eight-and-forty, who sat so heavily upon his gelding. The child, his darling Betty: there lay the root of his trouble. He was unhappy when near his wife, he was unhappy when away from his little girl, and from this dilemma there was no practicable escape. As a consequence, he indulged rather freely in the pleasures of the table, became what was called a three-bottle man, and, in his wife's estimation, less and less presentable to her polite friends from town.

lie was received by the two or three old servants who were in charge of the lonely place, where a few rooms only were kept habitable for his use or that of his friends when hunting ; and during the morning he was made more comfortable by the arrival of his faithful servant Tupcombe from King's-IIintock. But after a day or two spent

here in solitude he began to feel that he had made a mistake in coming. By leaving King's-Hintock in his anger he had thrown away his best opportunity of counteracting his wife's preposterous notion of promising his poor little Betty's hand to a man she had hardly seen. To protect her from such a repugnant bargain he should have remained on the spot. He felt it almost as a misfortune that the child would inherit so much wealth. She would be a mark for all the adventurers in the kingdom. Had she been only the heiress to his own unassuming little place at Falls, how much better would have been her chances of happiness!

His wife had divined truly when she insinuated that he himself had a lover in view for this pet child. The son of a dear deceased friend of his, who lived not two miles from where the Squire now was, a lad a couple of years his daughter's senior, seemed in her father's opinion the one person in the world likely to make her happy. But as to breathing such a scheme to either of the young people with the indecent haste that his wife had shown, he would not dream of it; years hence would be soon enough for that. They had already seen each other, and the Squire fancied that he noticed a tenderness on the youth's part which promised well. He was strongly tempted to profit by his wife's example, and forestall her match-making by throwing the two young people together there at Falls. The girl, though mar-

FALLS-PARK.

riageable in the views of those days, was too young to be in love, but the lad was fifteen, and already felt an interest in her.

Still better than keeping watch over her at King's-Hintock, where she was necessarily much under her mother's influence, would it be to get the child to stay with him at Falls for a time, under his exclusive control. But how accomplish this without using main force? The only possible chance was that his wife might, for appearance' sake, as she had done before, consent to Betty paying him a day's visit, when he might find means of detaining her until Reynard, the suitor whom his wife favored, had gone abroad, w^hich he was expected to do the following week. Squire Dornell determined to return to King's-Hintock and attempt the enterprise. If he Avere refused, it was almost in him to pick up Betty bodily and carry her off.

The journey back, vague and quixotic as were his intentions, was performed with a far lighter heart than his setting forth. He would see Betty and talk to her, come what might of his plan.

So he rode along the dead level which stretches between the hills skirting Falls-Park and those bounding the town of Ivell, trotted through that borough, and out by the King's-Hintock highway, till, passing the village, he entered the mile-long drive through the park to the Court. The drive being open, without an avenue, the Squire could discern the north front and door of the Court a long way off, and was himself visible from the windows on that side; for which reason he hoped that Betty might perceive him coming, as she sometimes did on his return from an outing, and run to the door or wave her handkerchief.

But there was no sign. He inquired for his wife as soon as he set foot to earth.

" Mistress is away. She was called to London, sir."

" And Mistress Betty?" said the Squire, blankly.

" Gone likewise, sir, for a little change. Mistress has left a letter for you."

The note explained nothing, merely stating that she had posted to London on her own affairs, and had taken the child to give her a holiday. On the fly-leaf were some words from Betty herself to the same effect, evidently written in a state of high jubilation at the idea of her jaunt. Squire Dornell murmured a few expletives, and submitted to his disappointment. How long his wife meant to stay in town she did not say; but on investigation he found that the cairiage had been packed with sufficient luggage for a sojourn of two or three weeks.

King's-Hintock Court was in consequence as gloomy as Falls-Park had been. He had lost all zest for hunting of late, and had hardly attended a meet that season. Dornell read and reread Betty's scrawl, and hunted up some other such notes of hers to look over, this seeming to be the only pleasure there was left for bim. That they were really in London he learned in a few days by another letter from Mrs. Dornell, in which she explained that they hoped to be home in about a week, and that she had had no idea he was coming back to King's-Hintock so soon, or she would not have gone away without telling him.

Squire Dornell wondered if, in going or returning, it had been her plan to call at the Reynards' place, near Melchester, through which city their journey lay. It was possible that she might do this in furtherance of her project, and the sense that his own might become the losing game was harassing.

He did not know how to dispose of himself, till it occurred to him that, to get rid of his intolerable heaviness, he would invite some friends to dinner and drown his cares in grog and wine. No sooner was the carouse decided upon than he put it in hand; those invited being mostly neighboring landholders, all smaller men than himself, members of the hunt; also the doctor from Evers-head, and the like — some of them rollicking blades whose presence his wife would not have countenanced had she been at home. " When the cat's away— " said the Squire.

They arrived, and there were indications in their manner that they meant to make a night of it. Baxby of Sherton Castle was late, and they waited a quarter of an hour for him, he being one of the liveliest of Dorueirs friends; without whose presence no such dinner as this would be considered complete, and, it may be added, with whose presence no dinner which included both sexes could be conducted with strict propriety. He had just returned from London, and the Squire was anxious to talk to him—for no definite reason; but he had lately breathed the atmosphere in which Betty was.

At length they heard Baxby driving up to the door, whereupon the host and the rest of his guests crossed over to the dining-room. In a moment Baxby came hastily in at their heels, apologizing for his lateness.

" I only came back last night, you know," he said; "and the truth o't is, I had as much as I could carry." He turned to the Squire. " Well, Dornell—so cunning Reynard has stolen your little ewe lamb ? Ha, ha !"

" What ?" said Squire Dornell, vacantly, across the dining-table, round which they were all standing, the cold March sunlight streaming in upon his full, clean-shaven face.

"Surely th'st know what all the town knows? —you've had a letter by this time?—that Stephen Reynard has married your daughter Betty ? Yes, as I'm a living man. It was a carefully-arranged thing ; they parted at once, and are not to meet for five or six years. But, Lord, you must know!"

A thud on the floor was the only reply of the Squire. They quickly turned. He had fallen down like a log behind the table, and lay motionless on the oak boards.

Those at hand hastily bent over him, and the whole group were in confusion. They found him to be quite unconscious, though puffing and panting like a blacksmith's bellows. His face was livid, his veins swollen, and beads of perspiration stood upon his brow.

" What's happened to him ?" said several.

"An apoplectic fit," said the doctor from Evers-head, gravely.

He was only called in at the Court for small ailments, as a rule, and felt the importance of the situation. He lifted the Squire's head, loosened his cravat and clothing, and rang for the servants, who took the Squire up-stairs.

There he lay as if in a drugged sleep. The surgeon drew a basinful of blood from Iiim, but it was nearly six o'clock before he came to himself. Tlie dinner was completely disorganized, and some had gone homo long ago; but two or three remained.

"Bless my soul," Baxby kept repeating, "I didn't know things had come to this pass between Dornell and his lady ! I thought the feast he was spreading to-day was in honor of the event, though privately kept for the present! His little maid married without his knowledge!"

As soon as the Squire recovered consciousness he gasped : "'Tis abduction ! 'Tis a capital felony ! He can be hung ! Where is Baxby ? I

am very well now. What items have ye heard, Baxby ?"

The bearer of the untoward news was extremely unwilling to agitate Dornell further, and would say little more at first. But an hour after, when the Squire had partially recovered and was sitting up, Baxby told as much as he knew, the most important particular being that Betty's mother was present at the marriage, and showed every mark of approval. " Everything appeared to have been done so regularly that I, of course, thought you knew all about it," he said.

"I knew no more than the underground dead that such a step was in the wind ! A child not yet thirteen ! How Sue hath outwitted me ! Did Reynard go up to Lon'on with 'em, d'ye know?"

" I can't say. All I know is that your lady and daughter were walking along the street, with the footman behind 'em; that they entered a jeweller's shop, where Reynard was standing ; and that there, in the presence o' the shopkeeper and your man, who was called in on purpose, your Betty said to Reynard—so the story goes : 'pon my soul, I don't vouch for the truth of it—she said, * Will you marry me ?' or, ' I want to marry you : will you have me—now or never?' she said."

" What she said means nothing," murmured the Squire, with wet eyes. "Her mother put the words into her mouth to avoid the serious consequences that would attach to any suspicion of force. The words be not the child's—she didn't

dream of marriage—liow should she, poor little maid ! Go on."

" Well, be that as it will, they were all agreed apparently. They bought the ring on the spot, and the marriage took place at the nearest church Avithin half an hour."

A day or two later there came a letter from Mrs. Dornell to her husband, written before she knew of his stroke. She related the circumstances of the raai'riage in the gentlest manner, and gave cogent reasons and excuses for consenting to the preraatui'e union, which was now an accomplished fact indeed. She had no idea, till sudden pressure was put upon her, that the contract was expected to be carried out so soon, but being taken half unawares, she had consented, having learned that Stephen Reynard, now their son-in-law, was becoming a great favorite at Court, and that he would in all likelihood have a title granted him before long. No harm could come to their dear daughter by this early marriage-contract, seeing that her life would be continued under their own eyes, exactly as before, for some years. In fine, she had felt that no other such fair opportunity for a good marriage with a shrewd courtier and wise man of the world, who was at the same time noted for his excellent personal qualities, was within the range of probability, owing to the rusticated lives they led at King's-Hintock. Hence she had yielded to Stephen's solicitations, and hoped

her husband would forgive her. She wrote, in short, like a woman who, having had her way as to the deed, is prepared to make any concession as to words and subsequent behavior.

All this Dornell took at its true value, or rather, perhaps, at less than its true value. As his life depended on his not getting into a passion, he controlled his perturbed emotions as well as he was able, going about the house sadly and utterly unlike his former self. He took every precaution to prevent his wife knowing of the incidents of his sudden illness, from a sense of shame at having a heart so tender ; a ridiculous quality, no doubt, in her eyes, now that she had become so imbued with town ideas. But rumors of his seizure somehow reached her, and she let him know that she was about to return to nurse him. He thereupon packed up and went off to his own place at Falls-Park.

Here he lived the life of a recluse for some time. He was still too unwell to entertain company, or to ride to hounds or elsewhither; but more than this, his aversion to the faces of strangers and acquaintances, who knew by that time of the trick his wife had played him, operated to hold him aloof.

Nothing could influence him to censure Betty for her share in the exploit. He never once believed that she had acted voluntarily. Anxious to know how she was getting on, he despatched the trusty servant Tupcombe to Evershead village,

THE FIRST COUNTESS OF WESSEX.

15

AT THE SOW-AND-ACORN.

close to King's-Hintock, timing his journey so tliat he slioukl reach the place under cover of (lark. The emissary arrived without notice, being out of livery, and took a seat in the chimney-corner of the Sow-and-Acorn.

The conversation of the droppers-in was always of the nine days' wonder — the recent marriage. The smoking listener learned that Mrs. Dornell and the girl had returned to King's-Hintock for a day or two, that Reynard had set out for the Continent, and that Betty had since been packed off to school. She did not realize her position as Reynard's child-wife—so the story went—and though somewhat awe-stricken at first by the ceremony, she had soon recovered her spirits on finding that her freedom was in no way to be interfered with.

After that, formal messages began to pass between Dornell and his wife, the latter being now as persistently conciliating as she was formerly masterful. But her rustic, simple, blustering husband still held personally aloof. Her wish to be reconciled—to win his forgiveness for her stratagem—moreover, a genuine tenderness and desire to soothe his sorrow, which welled up in her at times, brought her at last to his door at Falls-Park one day.

They had not met since that night of altercation, before her departure for London and his subsequent illness. She was shocked at the change in him. His face had become expressionless, as blank as that of a puppet, and what troubled her still more was that she found him living in one room, and indulging freely in stimulants, in absolute disobedience to the physician's order. The fact was obvious that he could no longer be allowed to live thus uncouthly.

So she sympathized, and begged his pardon, and coaxed. But though after this date there was no longer such a complete estrangement as before, they only occasionally saw each other, Dornell for the most part making Falls his headquarters still.

Three or four years passed thus. Then she came one day, with more animation in her manner, and at once moved him by the simple statement that Betty's schooling had ended; she had returned, and was grieved because he was away. She had sent a message to him in these words : " Ask father to come home to his dear Betty."

"Ah! Then she is very unhappy !" said Squire Dornell.

His wife was silent.

" 'Tis that accursed marriage !" continued the Squire.

Still his wife would not dispute with him. "She is outside in the carriage," said Mrs. Dornell, gently.

"What—Betty?"

"Yes."

" Why didn't you tell me ?" Dornell rushed out, and there was the girl awaiting liis forgiveness, for she supposed herself, no less than her mother, to be under his displeasure.

Yes, Betty had left school, and had returned to King's-Ilintock. She was nearly seventeen, and had developed to quite a young woman. She looked not less a member of the household for her early marriage-contract, which she seemed, indeed, to have almost forgotten. It was like a dream to her; that clear, cold March day, the London church, with its gorgeous pews and green-baize linings, and the great organ in the west gallery—so different from their own little church in the shrubbery of King's -Hintock Court—the man of thirty, to whose face she had looked up with so much awe, and with a sense that he was rather ugly and formidable ; the man whom, though they corresponded politely, she had never seen since ; one to whose existence she was now so indifferent that if informed of his death, and that she would never see him more, she would merely have replied, " Indeed !" Betty's passions as yet still slept.

"Hast heard from thy husband lately?" said Squire Dornell, when they were in-doors, with an ironical laugh of fondness which demanded no answer.

The girl winced, and he noticed that his wife looked appealingly at him. As the conversation went on, and there were signs that Dornell would express sentiments that might do harm to a position which they could not alter, Mrs. Dornell suggested that Betty should leave the room till her father and herself had finished their private conversation ; and this Betty obediently did.

Dornell renewed his animadversions freely. " Did you see how the sound of his name frightened her ?" he presently added. " If you didn't, I did. Zounds ! what a future is in store for that poor little unfortunate wench o' mine! I tell 'ee,

Suey 'twas not a marriage at all, in morality, and if I were a woman in such a position, I shouldn't feel it as one. She might, without a sign of sin, love a man of her choice as well now as if she were chained up to no other at all. There, that's my mind, and I can't help it. Ah, Sue, my man was best ! He'd ha' suited her."

"I don't believe it," she replied, incredulously.

" You should see him ; then you would. He's growing up a fine fellow, I can tell 'ee."

" Hush! not so loud !" she answered, rising from her seat and going to the door of the next room, whither her daughter had betaken herself. To Mrs. Dornell's alarm, there sat Betty in a reverie, her round eyes fixed on vacancy, musing so deeply that she did not perceive her mother's entrance. She had heard every word, and was digesting the new knowledge.

Her mother felt that Falls-Park was dangerous ground for a young girl of the susceptible age, and in Betty's peculiar position, while Dornell talked and reasoned thus. She called Betty to her, and they took leave. The Squire would not clearly promise to return and make King's-Hintock Court his permanent abode; but Betty's presence there, as at former times, was sufiicient to make him agree to pay them a visit soon.

All the way home Betty remained preoccupied and silent. It was too plain to her anxious mother that Squire Dornell's free views had been a sort of awakening to the girl.

The interval before Dornell redeemed his pledge to come and see them was unexpectedly short. He arrived one morning about twelve o'clock, driving his own pair of black bays in the curricle-phaeton with yellow panels and red wheels, just as he had used to do, and his faithful old Tup-combe on horseback behind. A young man sat beside the Squire in the carriage, and Mrs. Dor-nell's consternation could scarcely be concealed when, abruptly entering with his companion, the Squire announced him as his friend Phelipson of Elm-Cranlynch.

Dornell passed on to Betty in the background and tenderly kissed her. " Sting your mother's conscience, my maid !" he whispered. " Sting her conscience by pretending you are struck with Phelipson, and would ha' loved him, as your old father's choice, much more than him she has forced upon 'ee."

The simple-souled speaker fondly imagined that it was entirely in obedience to this direction that Betty's eyes stole interested glances at the frank and impulsive Phelipson that day at dinner, and he laughed grimly within himself to see how this joke of his, as he imagined it to be, was disturbing the peace of mind of the lady of the house. " Now Sue sees what a mistake she has made!" said he.

Mrs. Dornell was verily greatly alarmed, and as soon as she could speak a word with him alone she upbraided him. " You ought not to have brought him here. Oh, Thomas, how could you be so thoughtless! Lord, don't you see, dear, that what is done cannot be undone, and how all this foolery jeopardizes her happiness with her husband ? Until you interfered, and spoke in her hearing about this Phelipson, she was as patient and as willing as a lamb, and looked forward to Mr. Reynard's return with real pleasure. Since her visit to Falls-Park she has been monstrous close-mouthed and busy with her own thoughts. What mischief will you do ? How will it end ?"

" Own, then, that my man was best suited to her. I only brought him to convince you."

" Yes, yes ; I do admit it. But oh ! do take him back again at once ! Don't keep him here ! I fear she is even attracted by him already."

" Nonsense, Sue. 'Tis only a little trick to tease 'ce !"

Nevertheless her motherly eye was not so likely to be deceived as his, and if Betty were really only playing at being love-struck that day, she played it with the])erfection of a Rosalind, and would have deceived the best professors into a belief that it was no counterfeit. The Squire, having obtained his victory, was quite ready to take back the too attractive youth, and early in the afternoon they set out on their return journey.

A silent figure who rode behind them was as interested as Dornell in that day's experiment. It was the stanch Tupcombe, who, with his eyes on the Squire's and young Phelipson's backs, thought how well the latter would have suited Betty, and how greatly the former had changed for the worse during these last two or three years. He cursed his mistress as the cause of the change. After this memorable visit to prove his point, the lives of the Dornell couple flowed on quietly enough for the space of a twelvemonth, the Squire for the most part remaining at Falls, and Betty passing and repassing between them now and then, once or twice alarming her mother by not driving home from her father's house till midnight.

The repose of King's-Hintock was broken by the arrival of a special messenger. Squire Dornell had had an access of gout so violent as to be serious. He wished to see Betty again : why had she not come for so long?

Mrs. Dornell was extremely reluctant to take Betty in that direction too frequently ; but the girl was so anxious to go, her intei'ests latterly seeming to be so entirely bound up in Falls-Park and its neighborhood, that there was nothing to be done but to let her set out and accompany her.

Squire Dornell had been impatiently awaiting her arrival. They found him very ill and irritable. It had been his habit to take powerful medicines to drive away his enemy, and they had failed in their effect on this occasion.

The presence of his daughter, as usual, calmed him much, even while, as usual too, it saddened him; for he could never forget that she had disposed of herself for life in opposition to his wishes, though she had secretly assured him that she would never have consented liad she been as old as she was now.

As on a former occasion, bis wife wished to speak to him alone about the girl's future, tlie time now drawing nigh at which lleynard was expected to come and claim her. He would have done so already, but he had been put off by the earnest request of the young woman herself, which accorded with that of her parents, on the score of her youth. Reynard had deferentially submitted to their wishes in this respect, the understanding between them having been that he would not visit lier before she was eighteen, except by the mutual consent of all parties. But this could not go on much longer, and thei'e was no doubt, from the teror of his last letter, that he would soon take possession of her whether or no.

To be out of the sound of this delicate discussion Betty was accordingly sent down-stairs, and they soon saw her walking away into the shrubberies, looking very pretty in her sweeping green gown, and flapping broad-brimmed hat overhung with a feather.

On returning to the subject, Mrs. Dornell found her husband's reluctance to reply in the aftirmative to Reynard's letter to be as great as ever.

"She is three months short of ciglitcen !" he ex- claimed. " 'Tis too soon. I won't hear of it! If I have to keep him off sword in hand, he shall not have her yet."

" But, my dear Thomas," she expostulated, " consider if anything should happen to you or to me, how much better it would be that she should be settled in her home with him !"

*' I say it is too soon !" he argued, the veins of his forehead beginning to swell. " If he gets her this side o' Candlemas I'll challenge en—I'll take my oath on't! I'll be back at King's-Hintock in two or three days, and I'll not lose sight of her day or night!"

She feared to agitate him further, and gave way, assuring him, in obedience to his demand, that if Reynard should write again, before he got back, to fix a time for joining Betty, she would put the letter in her husband's hands, and he should do as he chose. This was all that required discussion privately, and Mrs. Dornell went to call in Betty, hoping that she had not heard her father's loud tones.

She had certainly not done so this time. Mrs. Dornell followed the path along which she had seen Betty wandering, but went a considerable distance without perceiving anything of her. The Squire's wife then turned round to proceed to the other side of the house by a short-cut across the grass, when, to her surprise and constei'nation, she beheld the object of her search sitting on the horizontal bough of a cedar, beside her being a

young man, whose arm was round her waist. He moved a little, and she recognized him as young Phelipson.

Alas, then, she was right! The so-called counterfeit love was real. What Mrs. Dornell called her husband at that moment, for his folly in originally throwing the young people together, it is not necessary to mention. She decided in a moment not to let the lovers know that she had seen them. She accordingly retreated, reached the front of the house by another route, and called at the top of her voice from a window, " Betty!"

For the first time since her strategic marriage of the child, Susan Dornell doubted the wisdom of that step. Her husband had, as it were, been assisted by destiny to make his objection, originally trivial, a valid one. She saw the outlines of trouble in the future. Why had Dornell interfered ? Why had hr. insisted upon producing his man ? This, then, accounted for Betty's pleading for postponement whenever the subject of her husband's return was broached ; this accounted for her attachment to Falls-Park. Possibly this very meeting that she had witnessed had been arranged by letter.

Perhaps the girl's thoughts would never have strayed for a moment if her father had not filled her head with ideas of repugnance to her early union, on the ground that she had been coerced into it before she knew her own mind; and she

might have rushed to meet her husband with open arms on the appointed day.

Betty at length appeared in the distance in answer to the call, and came up pale, but looking innocent of having seen a living soul. Mrs. Cornell groaned in spirit at such duplicity in the child of her bosom. This was the simple creature for whose development into womanhood they had all been so tenderly waiting — a forward minx, old enough not only to have a lover, but to conceal his existence as adroitly as any woman of the world! Bitterly did the Squire's lady regret that Stephen Reynard had not been allowed to come to claim her at the time he first proposed.

The two sat beside each other almost in silence on their journey back to King's-Hintock. Such words as were spoken came mainly from Betty, and their formality indicated how much her mind and heart were occupied with other things.

Mrs. Dornell was far too astute a mother to openly attack Betty on the matter. That would be only fanning flame. The indispensable course seemed to her to be that of keeping the treacherous girl under lock and key till her husband came to take her off her mother's hands. That he would disregard Dornell's opposition, and come soon, was her devout wish.

It seemed, therefore, a fortunate coincidence that on her arrival at King's-Hintock a letter from Reynard was put into Mrs, Dornell's hands. It was addressed to both her and her husband, and

courteously informed them that the writer had landed at Bristol, and proposed to come on to King's-Hintock in a few days, at last to meet and carry off his darling Betty, if she and her parents saw no objection.

Betty had also received a letter of the same tenor. Her mother had only to look at her face to see how the girl received the information. She was as pale as a sheet.

" You must do your best to welcome him this time, my dear Betty," her mother said, gently.

" But—but—I—"

"You are a woman now," added her mother, severely, " and these postponements must come to an end."

" But ray father—oh, I am sure he will not allow this! I am not ready. If he could only wait a year longer—if he could only wait a few months longer! Oh, I wish—I wish my dear father were here! I will send to him instantly." She broke off abruptly, and falling upon her mother's neck, burst into tears, saying, **0 my mother, have mercy upon me—I do not love this man, my husband 1"

The agonized appeal went too straight to Mrs, Dornell's heart for her to hear it unmoved. Yet, things having come to this pass, what could she do? She was distracted, and for a moment was on Betty's side. Her original thought had been to write an affirmative reply to Reynard, allow him to come on to King's-Hintock, and keep her

husband in ignorance of the whole proceeding till he should arrive from Falls on some fine day after his recovery, and find everything settled, and Reynard and Betty living together in harmony. But the events of the day, and her daughter's sudden outburst of feeling, had overthrown this intention. Betty was sure to do as she had threatened, and communicate instantly with her father, possibly attempt to fly to him. Moreover, Reynard's letter was addressed to Mr. Dornell and herself conjointly, and she could not in conscience keep it from her husband.

" I will send the letter on to your father instantly," she replied, soothingly. " He shall act entirely as he chooses, and you know that will not be in opposition to your wishes. He would ruin you rather than thwart you. I only hope he may be well enough to bear the agitation of this news. Do you agree to this?"

Poor Betty agreed, on condition that she should actually witness the despatch of the letter.

Her mother had no objection to offer to this; but as soon as the horseman had cantered down the drive towards the highway, Mrs. Dornell's sympathy with Betty's recalcitration began to die out. The girl's secret affection for young Phelipson could not possibly be condoned. Betty might communicate with him, might even try to reach him. Ruin lay that way. Stephen Reynard must be speedily installed in his proper place by Betty's side.

She sat down and penned a private letter to Reynard, which threw light upon her plan.

"It is necessary that I should now tell you," she said, " what I have never mentioned before— indeed I may have signified the contrary—that her father's objection to your joining her has not as yet been overcome. As I personally wish to delay you no longer—am indeed as anxious for your arrival as you can be yourself, having the good of my daughter at heart—no course is left open to me but to assist your cause without my husband's knowledge. He, I am sorry to say, is at present ill at Falls-Park, but I felt it my duty to forward him your letter. He will therefore be like to reply with a peremptory command to you to go back again, for some months, whence you came, till the time he originally stipulated has expired. My advice is, if you get such a letter, to take no notice of it, but to come on hither as you had proposed, letting me know the day and hour (after dark, if possible) at which we may expect you. Dear Betty is with me, and I warrant ye that she shall be in the house when you arrive."

Mrs. Dornell, having sent away tliis epistle unsuspected of anybody, next took steps to prevent her daughter leaving tlie Court, avoiding if possible to excite the girl's suspicions that she was under restraint. But, as if by divination, Betty had seemed to read the husband's approach in the aspect of her mother's face.

" He is coming !" exclaimed the maiden.

"Not for a week," her mother assured her,

" He is then—for certain ?"

" Well, yes."

Betty hastily retired to her room, and would not be seen.

To lock her up, and hand over the key to Reynard when he should appear in the hall, was a plan charming in its simplicity, till her mother found, on trying the door of the girl's chamber softly, that Betty had already locked and bolted it on the inside, and had given directions to have her meals served where she was, by leaving them on a dumbwaiter outside the door.

Thereupon Mrs. Dornell noiselessly sat down in her boudoir, which, as well as her bed-chamber, was a passage-room to the girl's apartment, and she resolved not to vacate her post night or day till her daughter's husband should appear, to which end she too arranged to breakfast, dine, and sup on the spot. It was impossible now that Betty should escape without her knowledge, even if she had wished, there being no other door to the chamber, except one admitting to a small inner dressing-room inaccessible by any second way.

But it was plain that the young girl had no thought of escape. Her ideas ran rather in the direction of intrenchment: she was prepared to stand a siege, but scorned flight. This, at any rate, rendered ber secure. As to how Reynard would contrive a meeting with her coy daughter Avhile in such a defensive humor, that, thought her mother, must be left to his own ingenuity to discover.

Betty had looked so wild and pale at the announcement of her husband's approaching visit, that Mrs. Dornell, somewhat uneasy, could not leave her to herself. She peeped through the keyhole an hour later. Betty lay on the sofa, staring listlessly at the ceiling.

" You are looking ill, child," cried her mother. " You've not taken the air lately. Come with me for a drive."

Betty made no objection. Soon they drove through the park towards the village, the daughter still in the strained, strung-up silence that had fallen upon her. Thej^ left the park to return by another route, and on the open road passed a cottage.

Betty's eye fell upon the cottage window. Within it she saw a young girl about her own age, whom she knew by sight, sitting in a chair and propped by a pillow. The girl's face was covered with scales, which glistened in the sun. She was a convalescent from small-pox—a disease whose prevalence at that period was a terror of which we at present can hardly form a conception.

An idea suddenly energized Betty's ajiathetic features. She glanced at her mother; Mrs. Dornell had been looking in the opposite direction.

Betty said that she wished to go back to the cottage for a moment to speak to a girl in whom she took an interest. Mrs. Dornell appeared suspicious, but observing that the cottage had no back-door, and that Betty could not escape without being seen, she allowed the carriage to be stopped. Betty ran back and entered the cottage, emerging again in about a minute, and resuming her seat in the carriage. As they drove on she fixed her eyes upon her mother and said, " There, I have done it now!" Her pale face was stormy, and her eyes full of waiting tears.

" What have you done ?" said Mrs. Dornell.

*' Nanny Priddle is sick of the small-pox, and 1 saw her at the window, and I went in and kissed her, so that I might take it; and now I shall have it, and he won't be able to come near me !"

" Wicked girl!" cries her mother. " Oh, what am I to do ! What—bring a distemper on yourself, and usurp the sacred prerogative of God, because you can't palate the man you've wedded !"

The alarmed woman gave orders to drive home as rapidly as possible, and, on arriving, Betty, who was by this time also somewhat frightened at her own enormity, was put into a bath, and fumigated, and treated in every way that could be thought of to ward off the dreadful malady that in a rash moment she had tried to acquire.

There was now a double reason for isolating the rebellious daughter and wife in her own chamber, and there she accordingly remained for

I

the rest of the day, and the days that followed, till no ill results seemed likely to arise from her wilfulness.

Meanwhile the first letter from Reynard, announcing to Mrs. Dornell and her husband jointly that he was coming in a few days, had sped on its way to Falls-Park. It was directed under cover to Tupcombe, the confidential servant, with instructions not to put it into his master's hands till he had been refreshed by a good long sleep. Tupcombe much regretted his commission, letters sent in this way always disturbing the Squire ; but guessing that it would be infinitely worse in the end to withhold the news than to reveal it, he chose his time, which was early the next morning, and delivered the missive.

Tiie utmost effect that Mrs. Dornell had anticipated from the message was a peremptory order from her husband to Reynard to hold aloof a few months longer. What the Squire really did was to declare that lie would go himself and confront Reynard at IJristol, and have it out with him tliere by word of mouth.

"But, master," said Tupcombe, "you can't. You cannot get out of bed."

" You leave the room, Tupcombe, and don't say 'can't' before me. Have Jerry saddled in an houi'."

The long-tried Tupcombe thought his employer demented, so utterly helpless was his appearance just then, and he went out reluctantly. No sooner was he gone than the Squire, with great difficulty, stretched himself over to a cabinet by the bedside, unlocked it, and took out a small bottle. It contained a gout specific, against whose use be had been repeatedly warned by his regular physician, but whose warning he now cast to the winds.

He took a double dose, and waited half an hour. It seemed to produce no effect. He then poured out a treble dose, swallowed it, leaned back on his pillow, and waited. The miracle he anticipated had been worked at last. It seemed as though the second draught had not only operated with its own strength, but had kindled into power the latent forces of the first. He put away the bottle and rang up Tupcombe.

Less than an hour later one of the house-maids, who of course was quite aware that the Squire's illness was serious, was surprised to hear a bold and decided step descending the stairs from the direction of Mr. Dornell's room, accompanied by the humming of a tune. She knew that the doctor had not paid a visit that morning, and that it was too heavy to be the valet or any other manservant. Looking up, she saw Squire Dornell, fully dressed, descending towards her in his drab caped riding-coat and boots, with the swinging, easy movement of his prime. Her face expressed her amazement.

"What the devil beest looking at?" said the Squire. " Did you never see a man walk out of his house before, wench ?"

Resuming his humming—which was of a defiant sort—he proceeded to the library, rang the bell, asked if the horses were ready, and directed them to be brought round. Ten minutes later he rode away in the direction of Bristol, Tupcombe behind him, trembling at what these movements might portend.

They rode on through the pleasant woodlands and the monotonous straight lanes at an equal pace. The distance traversed might have been about fifteen miles when Tupcombe could perceive that the Squire was getting tired—as weary as he would have been after riding three times the distance ten years before. However, they reached Bristol without any mishap, and put up at the Squire's accustomed inn, Dornell almost immediately proceeded on foot to the inn which Reynard had given as his address, it being now about four o'clock,

Reynard had already dined—for people dined early then — and he was staying in-doors. He had already received Mrs. Dornell's reply to his letter; but, before acting upon her advice and starting for King's-IIintock, he made up his mind to wait another day, that Betty's father might at least have time to write to him if so minded. The returned traveller much desired to obtain the Squire's assent, as well as his wife's, to the proposed visit to his bride, that nothing might seem harsh or forced in his method of taking his position as one of the family. But though he anticipated some sort of objection from his father-in-law, in consequence of Mrs. Dornell's warning, he was surprised at the announcement of the Squire in person.

Stephen Reynard formed the completest of possible contrasts to Dornell as they stood confronting each other in the best parlor of the Bristol tavern. The Squire, hot-tempered, gouty, impulsive, generous, reckless; the younger man, pale, tall, sedate, self-possessed—a man of the world, fully bearing out at least one couplet in his epitaph, still extant in King's-Hintock church, which places in the inventory of his good qualities

"Engaging Manners, cultivated Mind, Adoru'd by Letters, and in Courts refin'd."

He was at this time about five-and-thirty, though careful living and an even, unemotional temperament caused him to look much younger than his years.

Squire Dornell plunged into his errand without much ceremony or preface.

"I am your humble servant, sir," he said. "I have read your letter writ to my wife and myself, and considered that the best way to answer it would be to do so in person."

"I am vastly honored by your visit, sir," said Mr. Stephen Reynard, bowing.

"Well, what's done can't be undone," said Dornell, "though it was mighty early, and Avas no doing of mine. She's your wife; and there's an end on't. But in brief, sir, she's too young for you to claim yet; we mustn't reckon by years; we must reckon by nature. She's still a girl; 'tis onpolite of 'ee to come yet; next year will be full soon enough for you to take her to you."

Now, courteous as Reynard could bo, he was a little obstinate when his resolution had once been formed. She had been promised him by her eighteenth birthday at latest—sooner if she were in robust health. Her mother had fixed the time on her own judgment, without a Avord of interference on his part. He had been hanging about foreign courts till he was weary. Betty was now a woman, if she would ever be one, and there was not, in his mind, the shadow of an excuse for putting him off longer. Therefore, fortified as he was by the supi)ort of her mother, he blandly but firmly told the Squire that he had been willing to waive his rights, out of deference to her parents, to any reasonable extent, but must noAV, in justice to himself and her, insist on maintaining them. He therefore, since she had not come to meet him, should proceed to King's-Hiutock in a few days to fetch her.

This announcement, in spite of the urbanity Avith which it Avas delivered, set Dornell in a passion.

*' Oh dammy, sir; you talk about rights, you do, after stealing her aAvay, a mere child, against my will and knowledge! If we'd begged and prayed 'ee to take her, you could say no more."

"Upon my honor, your charge is quite baseless, sir," said his son-in-law. "You must know by this time—or if you do not, it has been a monstrous cruel injustice to me that I should have been allowed to remain in your mind with such a stain upon my character—you must know that I used no seductiveness or temptation of any kind. Her mother assented; she assented. I took them at their word. That you were really opposed to the marriage was not known to me till afterwards."

Dornell professed to believe not a word of it. "You sha'n't have her till she's dree sixes full— no maid ought to be married till she's dree sixes! —and my daughter sha'n't be treated out of na-ter!" So he stormed on till Tupcombe, who had been alarmedly listening in the next room, entered suddenly, declaring to Reynard that his master's life was in danger if the interview were prolonged, he being subject to apoplectic strokes at these crises. Reynard immediately said that he would be the last to wish to injure Squire Dornell, and left the room, and as soon as the Squire had recovered breath and equanimity, he went out of the inn, leaning on the arm of Tupcombe.

Tupcombe was for sleeping in Bristol that night, but Dornell, whose energy seemed as invincible as it was sudden, insisted upon mounting and getting back as far as Falls-Park, to continue the journey to King's-Hintock on the following day. At five they started, and took the southern road towards the Mendip Hills. The evening was dry and windy, and, excepting that the sun did not shine, strongly reminded Tupcombe of the evening of that March month, nearly five years earlier, when news had been brought to King's-Hintock Court of the child Betty's marriage in London—news which had produced upon Doruell such a marked e£Fect for the worse ever since, and indirectly upon the household of which he was the head. Before that time the winters were lively at Falls-Park, as well as at King's-Hintock, although the Squire had ceased to make it his regular residence. Hunting guests and shooting guests came and went, and open house was kept. Tupcombe disliked the clever courtier who had put a stop to this by taking away from the Squire the only treasure he valued.

It grew darker with their progress along the lanes, and Tupcombe discovered from Mr, Dor-nell's manner of riding that his strength was giving way; and spurring his own horse close alongside, he asked him how he felt,

" Oh, bad ; d bad, Tupcombe ! I can hardly keep my seat, I shall never be any better, I fear! Have we passed Three-Man-Gibbet yet?"

" Not yet by a long ways, sir,"

"I wish we had, I can hardly hold on." The Squire could not repress a groan now and then, and Tupcombe knew he was in great pain. " I wish I was underground—that's the place for such fools as I! I'd gladly be there if it were not for Mistress Betty. He's coming on to King's-Hintock to-morrow—he won't put it off any longer ; he'll set out and reach there to-moi*-row night, without stopping at Falls ; and he'll take her unawares, and I want to be there before him."

" I hope you may be well enough to do it, sir. But really—"

" I must, Tupcombe! You don't know what my trouble is ; it is not so much that she is married to this man without my agreeing—for, after all, there's nothing to say against him, so far as I know ; but that she don't take to him at all, seems to fear him—in fact, cares nothing about him; and if he comes forcing himself into the house upon her, why, 'twill be rank cruelty. Would to the Lord something would happen to prevent him !"

How they reached home that night Tupcombe hardly knew. The Squire was in such pain that he was obliged to recline uj^on his horse, and Tuj^combe was afraid every moment lest he would fall into the road. But they did reach home at last, and Mr. Dornell was instantly assisted to bed.

Next morning it was obvious that he could not possibly go to King's-Hintock for several days at least, and there on the bed he lay, cursing his inability to proceed on an errand so personal and so delicate that no emissary could perform it. What he wished to do Avas to ascertain from Betty's own lips if her aversion to Reynard was so strong that his presence would be positively distasteful to her. Were that the case, he would have borne her away bodily on the saddle behind him.

But all that was hindered now, and he repeated a hundred times in Tupcombe's hearing, and in that of the nurse and other servants, "I wish to God something would happen to him!"

This sentiment, reiterated by the Squire as he tossed in the agony induced by the powerful drugs of the day before, entered sharply into the soul of Tupcombe and of all who were attached to the house of Dornell, as distinct from the house of his Avife at King's-IIintoek. Tupcombe, who was an excitable man, was hardly less disquieted by the thought of Reynard's return than the

Squire himself was. As the week drew on, and the afternoon advanced at which Reynard would, in all probability, be i)assing near Falls on his way to the Court, the Squire's feelings became acuter, and the responsive Tui)combe could hardly bear to come near him. Ilaving left him in the hands of the doctor, the former went out upon the lawn, for he could hardly broatlie in the contagion of excitement caught from the employer who had virtually made him his confidant. He had lived with the Dornells from his boyhood, had been born under the shadow of their walls ;

his whole life was annexed and welded to the life of the family in a degree which has no counterpart in these latter days.

He was summoned in-doors, and learned that it had been decided to send for Mrs. Dornell; her husband was in great danger. There were two or three who could have acted as messenger, but Dornell wished Tupcombe to go, the reason showing itself when, Tupcombe being ready to start, Squire Dornell summoned him to his chamber and leaned down so that he could whisper in his ear :

"Put Peggy along smart, Tupcombe, and get there before him, you know—before him. This is the day he fixed. He has not passed Falls crossroads yet. If you can do that you will be able to get Betty to come—d'j^e see ?—after her mother has started ; she'll have a reason for not waiting for him. Bring her by the lower road — he'll go by the upper. Your business is to make 'em miss each other—d'ye see ?—but that's a thing I couldn't write down."

Five minutes after, Tupcombe was astride the horse and on his way—the way he had followed so many times since his master, a florid young countryman, had first gone wooing to King's-Hintock Court. As soon as he had crossed the hills in the immediate neighborhood of the manor, the road lay over a plain, where it ran in long, straight stretches for several miles. In the best of times, when all had been gay in the united

houses, that part of the road had seemed tedious. It was gloomy in the extreme now that he pursued it, at night and alone, on such an errand.

He rode and brooded. If the Squire were to die, he, Tupcombe, would be alone in the world and friendless, for he was no favorite with Mrs. Dornell; and to find himself bafiled, after all, in what he had set his mind on, would probably kill the Squire. Thinking thus, Tupcombe stopped his horse every now and then, and listened for the coming husband. The time was drawing on to the moment when Reynard might be expected to pass along this very route. He had Avatched the road well during the afternoon, and had inquired of the tavern-keepers as he came up to each, and he was convinced that the premature descent of the stranger-husband u]ion his young mistress had not been made by this highway as yet.

Besides the girl's mother, Tupcombe was the only member of the household who suspected Betty's tender feelings towards young Phelipson, so unhappily generated on her return from school; and he could therefore imagine, even better than her fond father, what would be her emotions on the sudden announcement of Reynard's advent that evening at King's-Ilintock Court.

So he rode and rode, desponding and hopeful by turns. He felt assured that, unless in the unfortunate event of the almost immediate arrival of her son-in-law at his own heels, Mrs. Dornell

would not be .able to hinder Betty's departure for her father's bedside.

It was about nine o'clock that, having put twenty miles of country behind him, he turned in at the lodge-gate nearest to Ivell and King's-Hintock village, and pursued the long north drive —itself much like a turnpike road—which led thence through the park to the Court. Though there were so many trees in King's-Hintock park, few bordered the carriage roadway ; he could see it stretching ahead in the pale night light like an unrolled deal shaving. Presently the irregular frontage of the house came in view, of great extent, but low, except where it rose into the outlines of a broad, square tower.

As Tupcombe approached he rode aside upon the grass, to make sure, if possible, that he was the first comer, before letting his presence be known. The Court was dark and sleepy, in no respect as if a bridegroom were about to arrive.

While pausing he distinctly heard the tread of a horse upon the track behind him, and for a moment despaired of arriving in time : here, surely, was Reynard ! Pulling up closer to the densest tree at hand he waited, and found he had retreated none too soon, for the second rider avoided the gravel also, and passed quite close to him. In the profile he recognized young Phe-lipson.

Before Tupcombe could think what to do, Phe-lipson had gone on; but not to the door of the

house. Swerving to the left, he passed round to the east angle, where, as Tupcombe knew, were situated Betty's apartments. Dismounting, he left the horse tethered to a hanging bough, and walked on to the house.

Suddenly his eye caught sight of an object which explained the position immediately. It was a ladder stretching from beneath the trees, which there came pretty close to the house, up to a first-floor window—one which lighted Miss Betty's rooms. Yes, it was Betty's chamber ; he knew every room in the house well.

The young horseman who had passed him, having evidently left his steed somewhere under the trees also, was perceptible at the top of the ladder, immediately outside Betty's window. While Tupcombe watched, a cloaked female figure stepped timidly o\er the sill, and the two cautiously descended, one before the other, the young man's arras enclosing the young woman between his grasp of the ladder, so that she could not fall. As soon as they reached the bottom, young Phelipson quickly removed the ladder and hid it under the bushes. The pair disappeared; till, in a few minutes, Tupcombe could discern a horse emerging from a remoter part of the umbrage. The horse carried double, the girl being on a pillion behind her lover.

Tupcombe hardly knew what to do or think ; yet, though this was not exactly the kind of flight that had been intended, she had certainly escaped.

He went back to his own animal, and rode round to the servants' door, where he delivered the letter for Mrs. Dornell. To leave a verbal message for Betty was now impossible.

The Court servants desired him to stay over the night, but he would not do so, desiring to get back to the Squire as soon as possible and tell what he had seen. Whether he ought not to have intercepted the young people, and carried off Betty himself to her father, he did not know. However, it was too late to think of that now, and without wetting his lips or swallowing a crumb, Tupcombe turned his back upon King's-Hintock Court.

It was not till he had advanced a considerable distance on his way homeward that, halting under the lantern of a road-side inn while the horse was watered, there came a traveller from the opposite direction in a hired coach ; the lantern lit the stranger's face as he passed along and dropped into the shade. Tupcombe exulted for the moment, though he could hardly have justified his exultation. The belated traveller was Reynard ; and another had stepped in before him.

You may now be willing to know of the fortunes of Miss Betty. Left much to herself through the intervening days, she had ample time to brood over her desperate attempt at the stratagem of infection—thwarted, apparently, by her mother's promptitude. In what other way to gain time she could not think. Thus drew on the

day and the hour of the evening on which her husband was expected to announce himself.

At some period after dark, when she could not tell, a tap at the window, twice and thrice repeated, became audible. It caused her to start up, for the only visitant in her mind was the one whose advances she had so feared as to risk health and life to repel them. She crept to the window, and heard a whisper without,

" It is I—Charley," said the voice,

Betty's face fired Avith excitement. She had latterly begun to doubt her admirer's stanchness, fancying his love to be going off in mere attentions which neither committed him nor herself very deeply. She opened the window, saying, in a joyous whisper, " Oh, Charley; I thought you had deserted me quite !"

He assured her he had not done that, and that he had a horse in waiting, if she would ride off with him, " You must come quickly," he said ; "for Reynard's on the way!"

To throw a cloak round herself was the work of a moment, and assuring herself that her door was locked against a surprise, she climbed over the window-sill and descended with him as we have seen.

Her mother meanwhile, having received Tup-combe's note, found the news of her husband's illness so serious as to displace her thoughts of the coming son-in-law, and she hastened to tell her daughter of the Squire's dangerous condition, thinking of it might be desirable to take her to her father's bedside. On trying the door of the girl's room, she found it still locked. Mrs. Dornell called, but there was no answer. Full of misgivings, she privately fetched the old house-steward and bade him burst open the door—an order by no means easy to execute, the joinery of the Court being massively constructed. However, the lock sprang open at last, and she entered Betty's chamber, only to find the window unfastened and the bird flown.

For a moment Mrs. Dornell was staggered. Then it occurred to her that Betty might have privately obtained from Tupcombe the news of her father's serious illness, and, fearing she might be kept back to meet her husband, have gone off with that obstinate and biassed servitor to Falls-Park. The more she thought it over the more probable did the supposition appear ; and binding her own headman to secrecy as to Betty's movements, whether as she conjectured or otherwise, Mrs. Dornell herself prepared to set out.

She had no suspicion how seriously her husband's malady had been aggravated by his ride to Bristol, and thought more of Betty's affairs than of her own. That Betty's husband should arrive by some other road to-night, and find neither wife nor mother-in-law to receive him, and no explanation of their absence, was possible ; but never forgetting chances, Mrs. Dornell as she journeyed kept her eyes fixed upon the highway on the off-side, where, before she had reached the town of Ivell, the hired coach containing Stephen Reynard flashed into the lamplight of her own carriage.

Mrs. Dornell's coachman pulled up, in obedience to a direction she had given him at starting ; the other coach was hailed, a few words passed, and Reynard alighted and came to Mrs. Dornell's carriage-window.

" Come inside," says she. " I want to speak privately" to you. Why are you so late ?"

" One hinderance and another," says he. " I meant to be at the Court by eight at latest. My gratitude for your letter. I hope—"

" You must not try to see Betty yet," said she. "There be far other and newer reasons against your seeing her now than there were when I wrote."

The circumstances were such that Mrs. Dornell could not possibly conceal them entirely; nothing short of knowing some of the facts would prevent his blindly acting in a manner which might be fatal to the future. Moreover, there are times when deeper intriguers than Mrs. Dornell feel that they must let out a few truths, if only in self-indulgence. So she told so much of recent surprises as that Betty's heart had been attracted by another image than his, and that his insisting on visiting her now might drive the girl to desperation. " Betty has, in fact, rushed off to her father to avoid you," she said. " But, if you 4 wait, she will soon forget this young man, and you will have nothing to fear."

As a woman and a mother she could go no further, and Betty's desperate attempt to infect herself the week before as a means of repelling him, together with the alarming possibility that, after all, she had not gone to her father but to her lover, was not revealed,

" Well," sighed the diplomatist, in a tone unexpectedly quiet, " such things have been known before. After all, she may prefer me to him some day, when she reflects how very differently I might have acted than I am going to act towards her. But I'll say no more about that now. I can have a bed at your house for to-night ?"

"To-night, certainly. And you leave to-morrow morning early?" She spoke anxiously, for on no account did she wish him to make further discoveries. " My husband is so seriously ill," she continued, " that my absence and Betty's on your arrival is naturally accounted for."

He promised to leave early, and to write to her soon. " And when I think the time is ripe," he said, "I'll write to her. I may have something to tell her that will bring her to gracious-ness."

It was about one o'clock in the morning when Mrs. Dornell reached Falls-Park. A double blow awaited her there. Betty had not arrived ; her flight had been elsewhither; and her stricken mother divined with whom. She ascended to the bedside of her husband, where, to her concern, she found that the physician had given up all hope. The Squire was sinking, and his extreme weakness had almost changed his character, except in the particular that his old obstinacy sustained him in a refusal to see a clergyman. He shed tears at the least word, and sobbed at the sight of his wife. He asked for Betty, and it was with a heavy heart that Mrs. Dornell told him that the girl had not accompanied her.

" He is not keeping her away ?"

" No, no. He is going back—he is not coming to her for some time."

"Then what is detaining her—cruel, neglectful maid!"

" No, no, Thomas ; she is— She could not come."

"How's that?"

Somehow the solemnity of these last moments of his gave him inquisitorial power, and the too cold wife could not conceal from him the flight which had taken place from King's-Hintock that night.

To her amazement, the effect upon him was electrical.

" What—Betty—a trump after all ? Hurrah ! She's her father's own maid ! She's game ! She knew he was her father's own choice ! She vowed that my man should win ! AVell done. Bet!— haw ! haw ! Hurrah !"

He had raised himself in bed by starts as he spoke, and now fell back exhausted. He never uttered another word, and died before the dawn. People said there had not been such an ungenteel death in a good county family for years.

Now I will go back to the time of Betty's riding off on the pillion behind her lover. They left the park by an obscure gate to the east, and presently found themselves in the lonely and solitary length of the old Roman road now called Long-Ash Lane.

By this time they were rather alarmed at their own performance, for they were both young and inexperienced. Hence they proceeded almost in silence till they came to a mean road-side inn which was not yet closed ; when Betty, who had held on to him with much misgivings all this while, felt dreadfully unwell, and said she thought she would like to get down.

They accordingly dismounted from the jaded animal that had brought them, and were shown into a small dark parlor, where they stood side by side awkwardly, like the fugitives they were. A light was brought, and when they were left alone Betty threw off the cloak which had enveloped her. No sooner did young Phelijoson see her face than he uttered an alarmed exclamation.

" Why, Lord, Lord, you are sickening for the small-pox !" he cried.

" Oh—I forgot!" faltered Betty. And then she informed him that, on hearing of her husband's approach the week before, in a desperate attempt to keep him from her side she had tried to imbibe the infection—an act which, till this moment, she had supposed to have been ineffectual, imagining her feverishness to be the result of her excitement.

The effect of this discovery upon young Phe-lipson was overwhelming. Better-seasoned men than he would not have been proof against it, and he was only a little over her own age. "And you've been holding on to me !" he said. "And suppose you get worse, and we both have it, what shall we do ? Won't you be a fright in a month or two, poor, poor Betty!"

In his horror he attempted to laugh, but the laugh ended in a weakly giggle. She was more woman than girl by this time, and realized his feeling.

" What—in trying to keep off him, I keep off you?" she said, miserably. "Do you hate me because I am going to be ugly and ill ?"

" Oh—no, no !" he said, soothingly. " But I—I am thinking if it is quite right for us to do this. You see, dear Betty, if you was not married it would be different. You are not in honor married to him we've often said ; still you are his by law, and you can't be mine while he's alive. And with this terrible sickness coming on, perhaps you had better let me take you back, and—climb in at the window again."

" Is this your love ?" said Betty, reproachfully.

" Oh, if you was sickening for the plague itself, and going to be as ugly as the Ooser in the church-vestry, I wouldn't—"

" No, no, you mistake, upon my soul!"

But Betty, with a swollen heart, had rewrapped herself and gone out of the door. The horse was still standing there. She mounted by the help of the upping - stock, and when he had followed her she said: "Do not come near me, Charley; but please lead the horse, so that if you've not caught anything already you'll not catch it going back. After all, what keeps off you may keep off him. Now onward."

He did not resist her command, and back they went by the way they had come, Betty shedding bitter tears at the retribution she had already brought upon herself ; for though she had reproached Phelipson, she was stanch enough not to blame him in her secret heart for showing that his love was only skin-deep. The hoi'se was stopped in the plantation, and they walked silently to the lawn, reaching the bushes wherein the ladder still lay.

" Will you put it up for me ?" she asked, mournfully.

He re-erected the ladder without a word; but when she approached to ascend he said, " Goodbye, Betty !"

"Good-bye!" said she, and involuntarily turned her face towards his. He hung back from imprinting the expected kiss, at which Betty started

as if she had received a poignant wound. She moved away so suddenly that he hardly had time to follow her up the ladder to prevent her falling.

"Tell your mother to get the doctor at once!" he said, anxiously.

She stepped in without looking behind ; he descended, withdrew the ladder, and went away.

Alone in her chamber, Betty flung herself upon her face on the bed, and burst into shaking sobs. Yet she would not admit to herself that her lover's conduct was unreasonable—only that her rash act of the previous week had been wrong. No one had heard her enter, and she was too worn out in body and mind to think or care about medical aid. In an hour or so she felt j^et more unwell, positively ill ; and nobody coming to her at the usual bedtime, she looked towards the door. Marks of the lock having been forced were visible, and this made her chary of summoning a servant. She opened the door cautiously and sallied forth down-stairs.

In the dining-parlor, as it was called, the now sick and sorry Betty was startled to see, at that late hour, not her mother, but a man sitting, calmly finishing his supper. There was no servant in the room. He turned, and she recognized her husband.

" Where's my mamma ?" she demanded, without preface.

" Gone to your father's. Is that—" He stopped, aghast.

"Yes, sir. This spotted object is your wife! I've done it because I don't want you to come near me!"

He was sixteen years her senior—old enough to be compassionate. "My poor child, you must get to bed directly! Don't be afraid of me— I'll carry you up-stairs and send for a doctor instantly."

"Ah, you don't know what I am!" she cried. "I had a lover once; but now he's gone! 'Twasn't I who deserted him; he has deserted me. Because I am ill he wouldn't kiss me, though I wanted him to!"

"Wouldn't he? Then he was a very poor, slack-twisted sort of fellow. Betty, I've never kissed you since you stood beside me as my little wife, twelve years and a half old! May I kiss you now?"

Though Betty by no means desired his kisses, she had enough of the spirit of Cunigonde, in Schiller's ballad, to test his daring. "If you have courage to venture, yes sir," said she. "But you may die for it, mind!"

He came up to her and imprinted a deliberate kiss full upon her mouth, saying, "May many others follow."

She shook her head, and hastily withdrew, though secretly pleased at his hardihood. The excitement had supported her for the few minutes she had passed in his presence, and she could hardly drag herself back to her room. Her husband summoned the servants, and, sending them to her assistance, went off himself for a doctor.

The next morning Reynard waited at the court till he had learned from the medical man that Betty's attack promised to be a very light one, or, as it was expressed, "very fine;" and in taking his leave sent up a note to her:

"Now I must be gone. I promised your mother I would not see you yet, and she may be angered if she finds me here. Promise to see me as soon as you are well?"

He was of all men then living one of the best able to cope with such an untimely situation as this. A contriving, sagacious, gentle-mannered man, a philosopher who saw that the only constant attribute of life is change, he held that, as long as she lives, there is nothing finite in the most impassioned attitude a woman may take up. In twelve months his girl-wife's recent infatuation might be as distasteful to her mind as it was now to his own. In a few years her very flesh would change—so said the scientific; her spirit, so much more ephemeral, was capable of changing in one. Betty was his, and it became a mere question of means how to effect that change.

During the day Mrs. Dornell, having closed her husband's eyes, returned to the Court. She was truly relieved to find Betty there, even though on a bed of sickness. The disease ran its course, and in due time Betty became convalescent, without having suffered deeply for her rashness, one little speck beneath her ear, and one beneath her chin, being all the marks she retained.

The Squire's body was not brought back to King's-Hintock. Where he was born, and where he had lived before wedding his Sue, there he had wished to be buried. No sooner had she lost him than Mrs. Dornell, like certain other wives, though she had never shown any great affection for him while he lived, awoke suddenly to his many virtues, and zealously embraced his opinion about delaying Betty's union with her husband, which she had formerly combated strenuously. "Poor man, how right he was, and how wrong was I!" Eighteen was certainly the lowest age at which Mr. Reynard should claim her child— nay, it was too low! Far too low!

So desirous was she of honoring her lamented husband's sentiments in this respect, that she wrote to her son-in-law suggesting that, partly on account of Betty's sorrow for her father's loss, and out of consideration for his known wishes for delay, Betty should not be taken from her till her nineteenth birthday.

However much or little Stephen Reynard might have been to blame in his marriage, the patient man now almost deserved to be pitied. First Betty's skittishness; now her mother's remorseful volte-face: it was enough to exasperate anybody; and he wrote to the widow in a tone which led to a little coolness between those hitherto firm friends. However, knowing that he had a wife

not to claim but to win, and that young Phelip-son had been packed off to sea by his parents, Stephen was complaisant to a degree, returning to London, and holding quite aloof from Betty and her mother, who remained for the present in the country. In town he had a mild visitation of the distemper he had taken from Betty, and in writing to her he took care not to dwell upon its mildness. It was now that Betty began to pity him for what she had inflicted upon him by the kiss, and her correspondence acquired a distinct flavor of kindness thenceforward.

Owing to his rebuffs, Reynard had grown to be truly in love with Betty in his mild, j^lacid, durable way—in that way which, perhaps, upon the whole, tends most generally to the woman's comfort under the institution of marriage, if not particularly to her ecstasy. Mrs. Dornell's exaggeration of her husband's wish for delay in their living together was inconvenient, but he would not openly infringe it. He wrote tenderly to Betty, and soon announced that he had a little surprise in store for her. The secret was that the King had been graciously pleased to inform him privately, through a relation, that His Majesty was about to offer him a Barony. Would she like the title to be Ivell ? Moreover, he had reasons for knowing that in a few years the dignity would be raised to that of an Earl, for which creation he thought the title of Wessex would be eminently suitable, considering the position of

much of their property. As Lady Ivell, therefore, and future Countess of Wessex, he should beg leave to offer her his heart a third time.

He did not add, as he might have added, how greatly the consideration of the enormous estates at King's-Hintock and elsewhere which Betty would inherit, and her children after her, had conduced to this desirable honor.

Whether the impending titles had really any effect upon Betty's regard for him I cannot state, for she was one of those close characters who never let their minds be known upon anything. That such honor was absolutely unexpected by her from such a quarter is, however, certain ; and she could not deny that Stephen had shown her kindness, forbearance, even magnanimity; had forgiven her for an errant passion which he might with some reason have denounced, notwithstanding her cruel position as a child entrapped into marriage ere able to understand its bearings.

Her mother, in her grief and remorse for the loveless life she had led with her rough, though open-hearted, husband, made now a creed of his merest whim; and continued to insist that, out of respect to his known desire, her son-in-law should not reside with Betty till the girl's father had been dead a year at least, at which time the girl would still be under nineteen. Letters must suffice for Stephen till then.

" It is rather long for him to wait," Betty hesitatingly said one day.

(I

"What!" said her mother. "From you? not to respect your dear father—"

" Of course it is quite proper," said Betty, hastily. " I don't gainsay it. I was but thinking that—that—"

In the long, slow months of the stipulated interval, her mother tended and trained Betty carefully for her duties. Fully awake now to the many virtues of her dear departed one, she, among other acts of pious devotion to his memory, rebuilt the church of King's-Hintock village, and established valuable charities in all the villages of that name, as far as to Little-Hintock, several miles eastward.

In superintending these works, particularly that of the church-building, her daughter Betty was her constant companion, and the incidents of their execution were doubtless not without a soothing effect upon the young creature's heart. She had sprung from girl to woman by a sudden bound, and few would have recognized in the thoughtful face of Betty now the same person who, the year before, had seemed to have absolutely no idea whatever of responsibility, moral or other. Time passed thus till the Squire had been nearly a year in his vault; and Mrs. Dornell was duly asked by letter by the patient Reynard if she were willing for him to come soon. He did not wish to take Betty away if her mother's sense of loneliness would be too great, but would willingly live at King's-Hintock a while with them.

Before the widow had replied to this communication, she one day happened to observe Betty walking on the south terrace in the full sunlight, without hat or mantle, and was struck by her child's figure. Mrs. Dornell called her in, and said, suddenly: " Have you seen your husband since the time of your poor father's death?"

" Well—yes, mamma," says Betty, coloring.

" What—against my wishes and those of your dear father! I am shocked at your disobedience!"

" But my father said eighteen, ma'am, and you made it much longer—"

"Why, of course—out of consideration for you! When have ye seen him?"

" Well," stammered Betty, " in the course of his letters to me he said that I belonged to him, and if nobody knew that we met it would make no difference. And that I need not hurt your feelings by telling you."

"Well?"

*' So I went to Casterbridge that time you went to London about five months ago—"

" And met him there ? When did you come back ?"

" Dear mamma, it grew very late, and he said it was safer not to go back till next day, as the roads were bad; and as you were away from home—"

" I don't want to hear any more ! This is your respect for your father's memory," groaned the widow. " When did you meet him again ?"

" Oh—not for more than a fortnight."

"A fortnight! How many times have ye seen him altogether ?"

"I'm sure, mamma, I've not seen him altogether a dozen times."

" A dozen ! And eighteen and a half years old barely !"

"Twice we met by accident," pleaded Betty. " Once at Abbot's-Cernel, and another time at the Red Lion, Melchester."

"Oh, thou deceitful girl!" cried Mrs. Dornell. " An accident took you to the Red Lion while I was staying at the White Hart! I remember— you came in at twelve o'clock at night, and said you'd been to see the cathedral by the light o' the moon!"

"My ever-honored mamma, so I had! I only went to the Red Lion with him afterwards."

" Oh Betty, Betty ! That my child should have deceived me even in my widowed days !"

"But, my dearest mamma, you made me marry him !" says Betty, with spirit, " and, of course, I've to obey him more tlian you now!"

Mrs. Dornell sighed. "All I have to say is, that you'd better get your husband to join you as soon as possible," she remarked. " To go on play-ins: the maiden like this — I'm ashamed to see you!"

She wrote instantly to Stephen Reynard: " I wash my hands of the whole matter as between you two; though I should advise you to openly join each other as soon as you can—if you wish to avoid scandal."

He came, though not till the promised title had been granted, and he could call Betty, archly," My Lady."

People said, in after-years, that she and her husband were very happy. However that may be, they had a numerous family; and she became in due course first Countess of Wessex, as he had foretold.

The little white frock in which she had been married to him, at the tender age of twelve, was carefully preserved among the relics at King's-Hintock Court, where it may still be seen by the curious—a yellowing, pathetic testimony to the small count taken of the happiness of an innocent child in the social strategy of those days, which might have led, but providentially did not lead, to great unhapj^iness.

When the earl died Betty wrote him an epitaph, in which she described him as the best of husbands, fathers, and friends, and called herself his disconsolate widow.

Such is woman; or, rather (not to give offence by so sweeping an assertion), such was Betty Dornell.

It was at a meeting of one of the "Wessex Field and Antiquarian clubs that the foregoing story, partly told, partly read from a manuscript, was made to do duty for the regulation papers on deformed butterflies, fossil ox-horns, prehistoric dung-mixens, and such like, that usually occupied the more serious attention of the members.

This club was of an inclusive and intersocial character; to a degree, indeed, remarkable for the part of England in which it had its being— dear, delightful Wessex, whose statuesque dynasties are even now only just beginning to feel the shaking of the new and strange spirit without, like that which entered the lonely valley of Ezeki-el's vision and made the dry bones move; where the honest squires, tradesmen, parsons, clerks, and people still j>raise the Lord with one voice for His best of all possible worlds.

The present niceting, which was to extend over two da^'s, had opened its proceedings at the museum of the town, whose buildings and environs were to be visited by the members. Lunch had ended, and the afternoon excursion had been about to be undertaken, when the rain came down in an obstinate spatter, which revealed no sign of cessation. As the members waited they grew chilly, although it was only autumn, and a fire was lighted, which threw a cheerful shine upon the varnished skulls, urns, penates, tesserai, costumes, coats of mail, weapons, and missals, animated the fossilized ichthyosaurus and iguanodon; while the dead eyes of the stuffed birds — those never-absent familiars in such collections, though murdered to extinction out of doors — flashed as they had flashed to the rising sun above the neighboring moors on the fatal morning when the trigger was pulled which ended their little flight. It was then that the historian produced his manuscript, which he had prepared, he said, with a view to publication. His delivery of the story having concluded as aforesaid, the speaker expressed his hope that the constraint of the weather, and the paucity of more scientific papers, would excuse any inappro-priateness in his subject.

Several members observed that a storm-bound club could not presume to be selective, and they were all very much obliged to him for siich a curious chapter from the domestic histories of the county.

The president looked gloomily from the window at the descending rain, and broke a short silence by saying that though the club had met, there seemed little probability of its being able to visit the objects of interest set down among the agenda.

The treasurer observed that they had at least a roof over their heads; and they had also a second day before them.

A sentimental member, leaning back in his chair, declared that he was in no hurry to go out, and that nothing would please him so much as another county story, with or without manuscript.

The colonel added that the subject should be a lady, like the former, to which a gentleman, known as the Spark, said " Hear, hear!"

Though these had spoken in jest, a rural dean

who was present observed blandly that there was no lack of materials. Many, indeed, were the legends and traditions of gentle and noble dames, renowned in times past in that part of England, whose actions and passions were now, but for men's memories, buried under the brief inscription on a tomb or an entry of dates in a dry pedigree.

Another member, an old surgeon, a somewhat grim though sociable personage, was quite of the speaker's opinion, and felt sure that the memory of the reverend gentleman must abound with such curious tales of fair dames, of their loves and hates, their joys and their misfortunes, their beauty and their fate.

The parson, a trifle confused, retorted that their friend the surgeon, the son of a surgeon, seemed to him, as a man who had seen much and heard more during the long course of his own and his father's practice, the member of all others most likely to be acquainted witli such lore.

The bookworm, the colonel, the historian, the vice-president, the churchwarden, the two curates, the gentleman-tradesman, the sentimental member, the crimson maltster, the quiet gentleman, the man of family, the Spark, and several others, quite agreed, and begged that he would recall something of the kind. The old surgeon said that, though a meeting of the Mid-Wessex Field and Antiquarian Club was the last place at which he should have expected to be called upon iu this

Cd A GROUP OF NOBLE DAMES.

way, he had no objection; and the parson said he would come next. The surgeon then reflected, and decided to relate the history of a lady named Barbara, who lived towards the end of the last century, apologizing for his tale as being perhaps a little too professional. The crimson maltster winked to the Spark at hearing the nature of the apology, and the surgeon began.

DAME THE SECOND.
Barbara, ot tbe Ibouse ot 0rebe.
BY THE OLD SURGEON.

It was apparently an idea, rather than a passion, that inspired Lord Uplandtowers' resolve to win her. Nobody ever knew when he formed it, or whence he got his assurance of success in the face of her manifest dislike of him. Possibly not until after that first important act of her life which I shall presently mention. His matured and cynical doggedness at the age of nineteen, when impulse mostly rules calculation, was remarkable, and might have owed its existence as much to his succession to the earldom and its accompanying local honors in childhood, as to the family character ; an elevation which jerked him into maturity, so to speak, without his having known adolescence. He had only reached his twelfth year when his father, the fourth earl, died, after a course of the Bath waters.

Nevertheless, the family character had a great ^eal to do with it. Determination was hereditary in the bearers of that escutcheon; sometimes for good, sometimes for evil.

The seats of the two families were about ten miles apart, the way between them lying along the now old, then new, turnpike-road connecting Havenpool and Warborne with the city of Mel-chester : a road which, though only a branch from what was known as the Great Western Highway, is probably, even at present, as it has been for the last hundred years, one of the finest examples of a macadamized turnpike-track that can be found in England.

The mansion of the earl, as well as that of his neighbor, Barbara's father, stood back about a mile from the highway, with which each was connected by an ordinary drive and lodge. It was along this particular highway that the young earl drove on a certain evening at Christmas-tide, some twenty years before the end of the last century, to attend a ball at Chene Manor, the home of Barbara and her parents, Sir John and Lady Grebe. Sir John's was a baronetcy created a few years before the breaking out of the Civil War, and his lands were even more extensive than those of Lord Uplandtowers himself, comprising this Manor of Chene, another on the coast near, half the Hundred of Cockdene, and well-enclosed lands in several other parishes, notably Warborne and those contiguous. At this time Barbara was barely seventeen, and the ball is the first occasion on which we have any tradition of Lord Upland-towers attemi->ting tender relations with her—it was early enough, God knows.

An intimate friend—one of the Drenkhards— is said to have dined with him that day, and Lord Uplandtowers had, for a wonder, communicated to his guest the secret design of his heart.

"You'll never get her—sure; you'll never get her!" this friend had said at parting. " She's not drawn to your lordship by love; and as for thought of a good match, why, there's no more calculation in her than in a bird."

" We'll see," said Lord Uplandtowers, impassively.

He no doubt thought of his friend's forecast as he travelled along the highway in his chariot; but the sculptural repose of his profile against the vanishing daylight on his right hand would have shown his friend that the earl's equanimity was undisturbed. He reached the solitary wayside tavern called Lornton Lin—the rendezvous of many a daring poacher for operations in the adjoining forest; and he might have observed, if he had taken the trouble, a strange post-chaise standing in the halting-space before the inn. He duly sped past it, and half an hour after through the little town of Warborne. Onward a mile farther was the house of his entertainer.

At this date it was an imposing edifice — or, rather, congeries of edifices—as extensive as the residence of the earl himself, though far less regular. One wing showed extreme antiquity, hav-ing huge chimneys, whose substructures projected from the external walls like towers; and a kitchen of vast dimensions, in which (it was said) breakfasts had been cooked for John of Gaunt. While he was yet in the forecourt he could hear the rhythm of French horns and clarionets, the favorite instruments of those days at such entertainments.

Entering the long parlor, in which the dance had just been opened by Lady Grebe with a minuet—it being now seven o'clock, according to the tradition — he was received with a welcome befitting his rank, and looked round for Barbara. She was not dancing, and seemed to be preoccupied— almost, indeed, as though she had been waiting for him. Barbara at this time was a good and pretty girl, who never spoke ill of any one, and hated other pretty women the very least possible. She did not refuse him for the country-dance which followed, and soon after was his partner in a second.

The evening wore on, and the horns and clarionets tootled merrily. Barbara evinced towards her lover neither distinct preference nor aversion, but old eyes would have seen that she pondered something. However, after supper she pleaded a headache, and disappeared. To pass the time of her absence, Lord Uplandtowers went into a little room adjoining the long gallery, where some elderly ones were sitting by the fire—for he had a phlegmatic dislike of dancing for its own sake

—and lifting the window-curtains, he looked out of the window into the park and wood, dark now as a cavern. Some of the guests appeared to be leaving even so soon as this, two lights showing themselves as turning away from the door and sinking to nothing in the distance.

His hostess put her head into tlie room to look for partners for the ladies, and Lord Uplandtow-ers came out. Lady Grebe informed him that Barbara had not returned to the ball-room ; she had gone to bed in sheer necessity.

" She has been so excited over the ball all day," her mother continued, "that I feared she would be worn out early. . . . But, sure. Lord Upland-towers, you won't be leaving yet ?"

He said that it was near twelve o'clock, and that some had already left.

" I protest nobody has gone yet," said Lady Grebe.

To humor her he stayed till midniglit, and then set out. He had made no progress in his suit; but he had assured himself that Barbara gave no other guest the preference, and nearly everybody in the neighborhood was there.

" 'Tis only a matter of time," said the calm young philosopher.

The next morning he lay till near ten o'clock, and he had only just come out upon the head of the staircase when he heard hoofs upon the gravel without ; in a few moments the door had been opened, and Sir John Grebe met him in the hall as he set foot on the lowest stair.

" My lord—where's Barbara—my daughter ?"

Even the Earl of Uplandtowers could not repress amazement. " What is the matter, my dear Sir John ?" says he.

The news was startling indeed. From the baronet's disjointed explanation Lord Upland-towers gathered that after his own and the other guests' departure Sir John and Lady Grebe had gone to rest without seeing any more of Barbara, it being understood by them that she had retired to bed when she sent word to say that she could not join the dancers again. Before then she had told her maid that she would dispense with her services for the night; and there was evidence to show that the young lady had never laid down at all, the bed being unpressed. Circumstances seemed to prove that the deceitful girl had feigned indisposition to get an excuse for leaving the ball-room, and that she had left the house within ten minutes—presumably during the first dance after supper.

" I saw her go," said Lord Uplandtowers.

" The devil you did !" says Sir John.

*' Yes." And he mentioned the retreating car-riage - lights, and how he was assured by Lady Grebe that no guest had departed,

"Surely that was it!" said the father. "But she's not gone alone, d'ye know!"

"Ah! Who is the young man?"

" I can on'y guess. My worst fear is my most likely guess. I'll say no more. I thought—yet I would not believe — it possible that you was the sinner. Would that you had been! But 'tis t'other, 'tis t'other, by G ! I must e'en up, and after 'em!"

" Whom do you suspect ?"

Sir John would not give a name, and, stultified rather than agitated, Lord Upland towers accompanied him back to Chene. lie again asked upon whom were the baronet's suspicions directed; and the impulsive Sir John was no match for the insistence of Uplandtowers.

He said, at length, "I fear 'tis Edmond Wil-lowes."

" Who's he ?"

"A young fellow of Shottsford - Forum — a widow-woman's son," the other told him, and ex-phiined that Willowes's father, or grandfather, was the last of the old glass - painters in that place, where (as you may know) the art lingered on when it had died out in every other part of England."

" By G , that's bad — mighty bad !" said

Lord Uplandtowers, throwing himself back in the chaise in frigid despair.

They despatched emissaries in all directions; one by the Melchester Road, another by Shotts-ford-Forum, another coastward.

But the lovers had a ten-hours' start; and it was apparent that sound judgment had been ex-

ercised in choosing as their time of flight the particular night when the movements of a strange carriage would not be noticed, either in the park or on the neighboring highway, owing to the general press of vehicles. The chaise which had been seen waiting at Lornton Inn was, no doubt, the one they had escaped in; and the pair of heads which had planned so cleverly thus far had probably contrived marriage ere now.

The fears of her parents were realized. A letter sent by special messenger from Barbara, on the evening of that day, briefly informed them that her lover and herself were on the way to London, and before this communication reached her home they would be united as husband and wife. She had taken this extreme step because she loved her dear Edmond as she could love no other man, and because she had seen closing round her the doom of marriage with Lord Uplandtow-ers, unless she put that threatened fate out of possibility by doing as she had done. She had well considered the step beforehand, and was prepared to live like any other country - townsman's wife if her father repudiated her for her action.

" D her !" said Lord Uplandtowers, as he

drove homeward that night. "D her for a

fool!"—which shows the kind of love he bore her.

Well, Sir John had already started in pursuit of them as a matter of duty, driving like a wild man to Melchester, and thence by the direct highway to the capital. But he soon saw that he was

acting to no purpose; and bj^-and-by, discovering that the marriage had actually taken place, he forebore all attempts to unearth them in the city, and returned and sat down with his lady to digest the event as best they could.

To proceed against this Willowes for the abduction of our heiress was, possibly, in their power; yet, when they considered the now unalterable facts, they refrained from violent retribution. Some six weeks passed, during which time Barbara's parents, though they keenly felt her loss, held no communication with the truant, either for reproach or condonation. They continued to think of the disgrace she had brought upon herself; for, though the young man was an honest fellow, and the son of an honest father, the latter had died so early, and iiis widow had had such struggles to maintain herself, that the son was very imperfectly educated. Moreover, his blood was, as far as they knew, of no distinction whatever, while hers, through her mother, was compounded of the best juices of ancient baronial distillation, containing tinctui-es of Maundeville, and Mohun, and Syward, and Peverell, and Culli-ford, and Talbot, and Plantagenet, and York, and Lancaster, and God knows what besides, which it was a thousand pities to throw away.

The father and mother sat by the fireplace that was spanned by the four-centred arch bearing the family shields on its haunches, and groaned aloud —the lady more than Sir John.

" To think this should have come upon us in our old age !" said he.

" Speak for yourself!" she snapped through her sobs. " I am only one-and-forty! . . . Why didn't ye ride faster and overtake 'em?"

In the mean time the young married lovers, caring no more about their blood than about ditch-water, were intensely happy—happy, that is, in the descending scale which, as we all know. Heaven in its wisdom has ordained for such rash cases; that is to say, the first week they were in the seventh heaven, the second in the sixth, the third week temperate, the fourth reflective, and so on; a lover's heart after possession being comparable to the earth in its geologic stages, as described to us sometimes by our worthy president; first a hot coal, then a warm one, then a cooling cinder, then chilly—the simile shall be pursued no further. The long and the short of it was that one day a letter, sealed with their daughter's own little seal, came into Sir John and Lady Grebe's hands; and, on opening it, they found it to contain an appeal from the young couple to Sir John to forgive them for what they had done, and they would fall on their naked knees and be most dutiful children for evermore.

Then Sir John and his lady sat down again by the fireplace with the four-centred arch, and consulted, and reread the letter. Sir John Grebe, if the truth must be told, loved his daughter's happiness far more, poor man, than he loved his name and lineage ; he recalled to liis raind all her little ways, gave vent to a sigh; and, by this time acclimatized to the idea of the marriage, said that what was done could not be undone, and that he supposed they must not be too harsh with her. Perhaps Barbara and her husband were in actual need; and how could they let their only child starve ?

A slight consolation had come to them in an unexpected manner. They had been credibly informed that an ancestor of plebeian Willowes was once honored with intermarriage with a scion of the aristocracy who had gone to the dogs. In short, such is the foolishness of distinguished parents, and sometimes of others also, that they wrote that very day to the address Barbara had given them, informing her that she might return home and bring her husband with her; they would not object to see him, would not reproach her, and would endeavor to welcome both, and to discuss with them what could best be arranged for their future.

In three or four days a rather shabby post-chaise drew up at the door of Chene Manor-house, at sound of which the tender-hearted baronet and his wife ran out as if to welcome a prince and princess of the blood. They were overjoyed to see their s\'7d)oilt child return safe and sound—though she was only I\Irs. Willowes, wife of Edmond Willowes of nowhere. Barbara burst into penitential tears, and both husband and wife were contrite enough, as well they might be, considering that they had not a guinea to call their own.

When the four had calmed themselves, and not a word of chiding had been uttered to the pair, they discussed the position soberly, young Wil-lowes sitting in the background with great modesty till invited forward by Lady Grebe in no frigid tone.

"How handsome he is!" she said to herself. "I don't wonder at Barbara's craze for him."

He was, indeed, one of the handsomest men who ever set his lips on a maid's. A blue coat, murrey waistcoat, and breeches of drab, set off a figure that could scarcely be surpassed. He had large, dark eyes, anxious now, as they glanced from Barbara to her parents and tenderly back again to her; observing whom, even now in her trepidation, one could see why the sang-froid of Lord Uplandtowers had been raised to more than lukewarmness. Her fair young face (according to the tale handed down by old women) looked out from under a gray conical hat, trimmed with white ostrich-feathers, and her little toes peeped from a buff petticoat worn under a puce gown. Her features were not regular; they were almost infantine, as you may see from miniatures in possession of the family, her mouth showing much sensitiveness, and one could be sure that her faults would not lie on the side of bad temper unless for urgent reasons.

Well, they discussed their state as became them, and the desire of the young couple to gain the good-will of those upon whom they were literally dependent for everything induced them to agree to any temj^orixing measure that was not too irksome. Therefore, having been nearly two months united, they did not oppose Sir John's proposal that he should furnish Edmond Willowes with funds sufficient for him to travel a year on the Continent in the company of a tutor, the young man undertaking to lend himself with the utmost diligence to the tutor's instructions, till he became polished outwardly and inwardly to the degree required in the husband of such a lady as Barbara. He was to apply himself to the study of languages, manners, history, society, ruins, and everything else that came under his eyes, till he should return to take his place without blushing by Barbara's side.

"And by that time," said worthy Sir John, "I'll get my little place out at Yewsholt ready for you and Barbara to occupy on your return. The house is small and out of the way; but it will do for a young couple for a while."

"If 'twere no bigger than a summer-house it would do!" says Barbara.

"If 'twere no bigger than a sedan-chair!" says Willowes. "And the more lonely the better."

"We can put up with the loneliness," said Barbara, with less zest. "Some friends will come, no doubt."

All this being laid down, a travelled tutor was called in—a man of many gifts and great experience—and on a fine morning away tutor and pupil went. A great reason urged against Barbara accompanying her youthful husband was that his attentions to her would naturally be such as to prevent his zealously applying every hour of his time to learning and seeing—an argument of wise prescience, and unanswerable. Regular days for letter-writing were fixed, Barbara and her Ed-mond exchanged their last kisses at the door, and the chaise swept under the archway into the drive.

He wrote to her from Le Havre, as soon as he reached that port, which was not for seven days, on account of adverse winds; he wrote from Rouen, and from Paris; described to her his sight of the King and Court at Versailles, and the wonderful marble-work and mirrors in that palace; wrote next from Lyons; then, after a comparatively long interval, from Turin, narrating his fearful adventures in crossing Mont Cenis on mules, and how he was overtaken with a terrific snow-storm, which had wellnigh been the end of him, and his tutor, and his guides. Then he wrote glowingly of Italy; and Barbara could see the development of her husband's mind reflected in his letters month by month; and she much admired the forethought of her father in suggesting this education for Edmond. Yet she sighed sometimes — her husband being no longer in evidence to fortify her in her choice of him—and timidly dreaded what mortifications might be in store for her by reason of this mesalliance. She went out very little; for on the one or two occasions on which she had shown herself to former friends she noticed a distinct difference in their manner, as though they should say, "Ah, my happy swain's wife; you're caught!"

Edmond's lettei's were as affectionate as ever; even more affectionate, after a while, than hers were to him. Barbara observed this growing coolness in herself; and like a good and honest lady was horrified and grieved, since her only wish was to act faithfully and uprightly. It troubled her so much that she prayed for a warmer heart, and at last wrote to her husband to beg him, now that he was in the land of Art, to send her his]>ortrait, ever so small, that she might look at it all day and every day, and never for a moment forget his features.

Willowes was nothing loath, and replied that be would do more than she wished ; he had made friends with a sculptor in Pisa, who was much interested in him and his history; and he had commissioned this artist to make a bust of himself in marble, which when finished he would send her. What Barbara had wanted was something immediate; but she expressed no objection to the delay; and in his next communication Edmond told her that the sculptor, of his own choice, had decided to increase the bust to a full-length statue, so anxious was he to get a specimen of his skill introduced to the notice of the English aristocracy. It was progressing well and rapidly.

Meanwhile, Barbara's attention began to be occupied at home with Yewsholt Lodge, the house that her kind-hearted father was preparing for her residence when her husband returned. It was a small place on the plan of a large one—a cottage built in the form of a mansion, having a central hall with a wooden gallery running round it, and rooms no bigger than closets to follow this introduction. It stood on a slope so solitary, and surrounded by trees so dense, that the birds who inhabited the boughs sang at strange hours, as if they hardly could distinguish night from day.

During the progress of repairs at this bower Barbara frequently visited it. Though so secluded by the dense growth, it was near the highroad, and one day while looking over the fence she saw Lord Uplandtowers riding past. He saluted her courteously, yet with mechanical stiffness, and did not halt. Barbara went home, and continued to pray that she might never cease to love her husband. After that she sickened, and did not come out of doors again for a long time.

The year of education had extended to fourteen months, and the house was in order for Edmond's return to take up his abode there with Barbara, Avhen, instead of the accustomed letter for her, came one to Sir John Grebe in the handwriting of the said tutor, informing him of a terrible catastrophe that had occurred to them at Venice.

Mr. Willowes and himself had attended the theatre one night during tlie Carnival of the preceding week, to witness the Italian comedy, when, owing to the carelessness of one of the candle-snuffers, the theatre had caught fire and been burned to the ground. Few persons had lost their lives, owing to the superhuman exertions of some of the audience in getting out the senseless sufferers; and, among them all, he who had risked his own life the most heroically was Mr. Willowes. In re-entering for the fifth time to save his fellow-creatures some fiery beams had fallen upon him, and he had been given up for lost. He was, however, by the blessing of Providence, recovered, with the life still in him, though he was fearfully burned; and by almost a miracle he seemed likely to survive, his constitution being wondrously sound. He was, of course, unable to write, but he was receiving the attention of several skilful surgeons. Further report would be made by the next mail or by private hand.

The tutor said nothing in detail of poor "Wil-lowes's sufferings, but as soon as the news was broken to Barbara she realized how intense they must have been, and her immediate instinct was to rush to his side, though, on consideration, the journey seemed impossible to her. Her health was by no means what it had been, and to post across Europe at that season of the year, or to traverse the Bay of Biscay in a sailing-craft, Avas

an undertaking that would hardly be justified by o

the result. But she was anxious to go till, on reading to the end of the letter, her husband's tutor was found to hint very strongly against such a step if it should be contemplated, this being also the opinion of the surgeons. And though Willowes's comrade refrained from giving his reasons, they disclosed themselves plainly enough in the sequel.

The truth was that the worst of the wounds resulting from the fire had occurred to his head and face — that handsome face which had won her heart from her—and both the tutor and the surgeons knew that for a sensitive young woman to see him before his wounds had healed would cause more misery to her by the shock than happiness to him by her ministrations.

Lady Grebe blurted out what Sir John and Barbara had thought, but had had too much delicacy to express.

"Sure,'tis mighty hard for you, poor Barbara, that the one little gift he had to justify your rash choice of him—his wonderful good looks—should be taken away like this, to leave 'ee no excuse at all for your conduct in the world's eyes. . . . Well, I wish you'd married t'other—that do I!" And the lady sighed.

"He'll soon get right again," said her father, soothingly.

Such remarks as the above were not often made; but they were frequent enough to cause Barbara an uneasy sense of self-stultification. She

determined to hear them no longer; and the house at Yewsholt being ready and furnished, she withdrew thither with her maids, where for the first time she could feel mistress of a home that would be hers and her husband's exclusively, when he came.

After long weeks Willowes had recovered sufficiently to be able to write himself, and slowly and tenderly he enlightened her upon the full extent of his injuries. It was a mercy, he said, that he had not lost his sight entirely; but he was thankful to say that he still retained full vision in one eye, though the other was dark forever. The sparing manner in which he meted out particulars of his condition told Barbara how appalling had been his experience. He was grateful for her assurance that nothing could change her; but feared that she did not fully realize that he was so sadly disfigured as to make it doubtful if she would recognize him. However, in spite of all, his heart was as true to her as it ever had been.

Barbara saw from his anxiety how much lay behind. She replied that she submitted to the decrees of Fate, and would welcome him in any shape as soon as he could come. She told him of the pretty retreat in which she had taken up her abode, pending their joint occupation of it, and did not reveal how much she had sighed over the information that all his good looks were gone.

Still less did she say that she felt a certain strangeness in awaiting him, the weeks they had lived together having been so short by comparison with the length of his absence.

Slowly drew on the time when Willowes found himself well enough to come home. He landed at Southampton, and posted thence towards Yewsbolt. Barbara arranged to go out to meet him as far as Lornton Inn—the spot between the Forest and the Chase at which he had waited for night on the evening of their elopement. Thither she drove at the appointed hour in a little pony-chaise, presented her by her father on her birthday for her especial use in her new house; which vehicle she sent back on arriving at the inn, the plan agreed upon being that she should perform the return journey with her husband in his hired coach.

There was not much accommodation for a lady at this way-side tavern; but, as it was a fine evening in early summer, she did not mind—walking about outside, and straining her eyes along the highway for the expected one. But each cloud of dust that enlarged in the distance and drew near was found to disclose a conveyance other than his post-chaise. Barbara remained till the appointment was two hours passed, and then began to fear that owing to some adverse wind in the Channel he was not coming that night.

While waiting she was conscious of a curious trepidation that was not entirely solicitude, and did not amount to dread; her tense state of incertitude bordered both on disappointment and on relief. She had lived six or seven weeks with an imperfectly educated yet handsome husband whom now she had not seen for seventeen months, and who was so changed physically by an accident that she was assured she would hardly know him. Can we wonder at her compound state of mind?

But her immediate difficulty was to get away from Lornton Inn, for her situation was becoming embarrassing. Like too many of Barbara's actions, this drive had been undertaken without much reflection. Expecting to wait no more than a few minutes for her husband in his post-chaise, and to enter it with him, she had not hesitated to isolate herself by sending back her own little vehicle. She now found that, being so well known in this neighborhood, her excursion to meet her long-absent husband was exciting great interest. She was conscious that more eyes were watching her from the inn windows than met her own gaze. Barbara had decided to get home by hiring whatever kind of conveyance the tavern afforded, when, straining her eyes for the last time over the now darkening highway, she perceived yet another dust-cloud drawing near. She paused; a chariot ascended to the inn, and would have passed had not its occupant caught sight of her standing expectantly. The horses were checked on the instant.

"You here—and alone, my dear Mrs. Willowes?" said Lord Uplandtowers, whose carriage it was.

She explained what had brought her into this lonely situation; and, as he was going in the direction of her own home, she accepted his offer of a seat beside him. Their conversation was embarrassed and fragmentary at first; but when they had driven a mile or two she was surprised to find herself talking earnestly and warmly to him: her impulsiveness was in truth but the natural consequence of her late existence—a somewhat desolate one by reason of the strange marriage she had made; and there is no more indiscreet mood than that of a woman surprised into talk who has long been imposing upon herself a policy of reserve. Therefore her ingenuous heart rose with a bound into her throat when, in response to his leading questions, or rather hints, she allowed her troubles to leak out of her. Lord Uplandtowers took her quite to her own door, although he had driven three miles out of his way to do so; and in handing her down she heard from him a whisper of stern reproach: " It need not have been thus if you had listened to me!"

She made no reply, and went in-doors. There, as the evening wore away, she regretted more and more that she had been so friendly with Lord Uplandtowers. But he had launched himself upon her so unexpectedly; if she had only foreseen the meeting with him, what a careful line of conduct she would have marked out! Barbara broke into a perspiration of disquiet when she thought of her unreserve, and, in self - chastise-

raent, resolved to sit up till midnight on the bare chance of Edmond's return ; directing that supper should be laid for him, improbable as his arrival till the morrow was.

The hours went past, and there was dead silence in and round Yewsholt Lodge, except for the soughing of the trees; till, when it was near upon midnight, she heard the noise of hoofs and wheels approaching the door. Knowing that it could only be her husband, Barbara instantly went into the hall to meet him. Yet she stood there not without a sensation of faintness, so many were the changes since their parting! And, owing to her casual encounter with Lord Uplandtowers, his voice and image still remained with her, excluding Edmond, her husband, from the inner circle of her impressions.

But she went to the door, and the next moment a figure stepped inside, of which she knew the outline, but little besides. Her husband was attired in a flapping black cloak and slouched hat, appearing altogether as a foreigner, and not as the young English burgess who had left her side. When he came forward into the light of the lamp, she perceived with surprise, and almost with fright, that he wore a mask. At first she had not noticed this — there being nothing in its color which would lead a casual observer to think he was looking on anything but a real countenance.

He must have seen her start of dismay at the unexpectedness of his appearance, for he said.

hastily: "I did not mean to come in to you like this—I thought you would have been in bed. How good you are, dear Barbara!" He put his arm round her, but he did not attempt to kiss her.

" Oh, Edmond—it is you ?—it must be ?" she said, with clasped hands, for though his figure and movement were almost enough to prove it, and the tones were not unlike the old tones, the enunciation was so altered as to seem that of a stranger.

" I am covered like this to hide myself from the curious eyes of the inn-servants and others," he said, in a low voice. " I will send back the cai'riage and join you in a moment."

" You are quite alone ?"

" Quite. My companion stopped at Southampton."

The wheels of the post-chaise rolled away a8 she entered the dining-room, where the supper was spread; and presently he rejoined her there. He had removed his cloak and hat, but the mask was still retained; and she could now see that it was of special make, of some flexible material like silk, colored so as to represent flesh; it joined naturally to the front hair, and was otherwise cleverly executed.

" Barbara—you look ill," he said, removing his glove, and taking her hand.

" Yes—I have been ill," said she.

" Is this pretty little house ours ?'*

"Oh—yes." She was hardly conscious of her

words, for the hand he had ungloved in order to take hers was contorted, and had one or two of its fingers missing; while through the mask she discerned the twinkle of one eye only.

"I would give anything to kiss you, dearest, now, at this moment!" he continued, with mournful passionateness. "But I cannot—in this guise. The servants are abed, I suppose?"

"Yes," said she, "But I can call them? You will have some supper?"

He said he would have some, but that it was not necessary to call anybody at that hour. Thereupon they approached the table, and sat down, facing each other.

Despite Barbara's scared state of mind, it was forced upon her notice that her husband trembled, as if he feared the impression he was producing, or was about to produce, as much as, or more than, she. He drew nearer and took her hand again.

"I had this mask made at Venice," he began, in evident embarrassment. "My darling Barbara —my dearest wife—do you think you—will mind when I take it off? You will not dislike me—will you?"

'* Oh, Edmond, of course I shall not mind," said she. " What has happened to you is our misfortune; but I am prepared for it."

"Are you sure you are prepared?"

** Oh yes. You are my husband."

"You really feel quite confident that nothing external can affect you?" he said again, in a voice rendered uncertain by his agitation.

"I think I am—quite," she answered, faintly.

He bent his head. "I hope—I hope you are," he whispered.

In the pause which followed, the ticking of the clock in the hall seemed to grow loud; and he turned a little aside to remove the mask. She breathlessly awaited the operation, which was one of some tediousness, watching him one moment, averting her face the next; and when it was done she shut her eyes at the hideous spectacle that was revealed. A quick spasm of horror had passed through her; but though she quailed she forced herself to regard him anew, repressing the cry that would naturally have escaped from her ashy lips. Unable to look at him longer, Barbara sank down on the floor beside her chair, covering her eyes.

"You cannot look at me!" he groaned, in a hopeless way. "I am too terrible an object even for you to bear! I knew it; yet I hoped against it. Oh, this is a bitter fate—curse the skill of those Venetian surgeons who saved me alive! . . . Look up, Barbara," he continued, beseechingly; " view me completely; say you loathe me, if you do loathe me, and settle the case between us forever!"

His unhappy wife pulled herself together for a desperate strain. He was her Edmond; he had done her no wrong; he had suffered. A momentary devotion to him helped her, and lifting her eyes as bidden, she regarded this human remnant, this ^corche, a second time. But the sight was too much. She again involuntarily looked aside and shuddered.

*'Do you think you can get used to this?" he said. " Yes or no! Can you bear such a thing of the charnel-house near you? Judge for yourself, Barbara. Your Adonis, your matchless man, has come to this!"

The poor lady stood beside him motionless, save for the restlessness of her eyes. All her natural sentiments of affection and pity were driven clean out of her by a sort of panic; she had just the same sense of dismay and fearfulness that she would have had in the presence of an apparition. She could nohow fancy this to be her chosen one —the man she had loved; he was metamorphosed to a specimen of another species. "I do not loathe you," she said, with trembling, "But I am so horrified—so overcome! Let me recover myself. Will you sup now? And while you do so may I go to my room to—regain my old feeling for you? I will try, if I may leave you a while? Yes, I will try !"

Without waiting for an answer from him, and keeping her gaze carefully averted, the frightened woman crept to the door and out of the room. She heard him sit down to the table, as if to begin supper; though, Heaven knows, his appetite was slight enough after a reception which had confirmed his worst surmises. When Barbara had ascended the stairs and arrived in her chamber she sank down, and buried her face in the coverlet of the bed.

Thus she remained for some time. The bedchamber was over the dining-room, and presently as she knelt Barbara heard Willowes thrust back his chair and rise to go into the hall. In five minutes that figure would probably come up the stairs and confront her again—it, this new and terrible form that was not her husband's. In the loneliness of this night, with neither maid nor friend beside her, she lost all self-control, and at the first sound of his footstep on the stairs, without so much as flinging a cloak round her, she flew from the room, ran along the gallery to the back staircase, which she descended, and, unlocking the back door, let herself out. She scarcely was aware what she had done till she found herself in the greenhouse, crouching on a flower-stand.

Here she remained, her great timid eyes strained through the glass upon the garden without, and her skirts gathered up, in fear of the field-mice which sometimes came there. Every moment she dreaded to hear footsteps which she ought by law to have longed for, and a voice that should have been as music to her soul. But Edmond Willowes came not that way. The nights were getting short at this season, and soon the dawn appeared, and the first rays of the sun.

By daylight she had less fear than in the dark. She thought she could meet him, and accustom herself to the spectacle.

So the much-tried young woman unfastened the door of the hot-house, and went back by the way she had emerged a few hours ago. Her poor husband was probably in bed and asleep, his journey having been long; and she made as little noise as possible in her entry. The house was just as she had left it, and she looked about in the hall for his cloak and hat, but she could not see them; nor did she perceive the small trunk which had been all that he brought with him, his heavier baggage having been left at Southampton for the road-wagon. She summoned courage to mount the stairs; the bedroom door was open as she had left it. She fearfully peeped round; the bed had not been pressed. Perhaps he had laid down on the dining-room sofa. She descended and entered; he was not there. On the table beside his unsoiled plate lay a note, hastily written on the leaf of a pocket-book. It was something like this:

"My Ever-beloved Wife,—The effect that my forbidding appearance has produced upon you was one which I foresaw as quite possible. I hoped against it, but foolishly so. I was aware that no human love could survive such a catastrophe. I confess I thought yours divine; but, after so long an absence, there could not be left sufficient warmth to overcome the too natural first aversion. It was an experiment, and it has failed. I do not blame you ; perhaps, even, it is better so. Good-bye. I leave England for one year. You will see me again at the expiration of that time, if I live. Then I will ascertain your true feeling ; and, if it be against me, go away forever. E. W."

On recovering from her surprise, Barbara's remorse was such that she felt herself absolutely unforgivable. She should have regarded him as an afflicted being, and not have been this slave to mere eyesight, like a child. To follow him and entreat him to return was her first thought. But on making inquiries she found that nobody had seen him ; he had silently disappeared.

More than this, to undo the scene of last night was impossible. Her terror had been too plain, and he was a man unlikely to be coaxed back by her efforts to do her duty. She went and confessed to her parents all that had occurred; which, indeed, soon became known to more per. sons than those of her own family.

The year passed, and he did not return; and it was doubted if he were alive. Barbara's contrition for her unconquerable repugnance was now such that she longed to build a church-aisle, or erect a monument, and devote herself to deeds of charity for the remainder of her days. To that end she made inquiry of the excellent parson un-

der whom she sat on Sundays at a vertical distance of twenty feet. But he could only adjust his wig and tap his snuffbox ; for such was the lukewarm state of religion in those days, that not an aisle, steeple, porch, east window, Ten-Cora-raandmcnt board, lion-and-unicorn, or brass candlestick, was required anywhere at all in the neighborhood as a votive offering from a distracted soul—the last century contrasting greatly in this respect with the haj)py times in which we live, when urgent appeals for contributions to such objects pour in by every morning's post, and nearly all churches have been made to look like new pennies. As the poor lady could not ease her conscience this way, she determined at least to be charitable, and soon had the satisfaction of finding her porch thronged every morning by the raggedest, idlest, most drunken, hypocritical, and worthless tramps in Christendom.

But human hearts are as prone to change as the leaves of the creeper on the wall, and in the course of time, hearing ncjthing of her husband Barbara could sit unmoved while her mother and friends said in her hearing, " Well, what has happened is for the best." She began to think so herself, for even now she could not summon up that lopped and mutilated form without a shiver, though whenever her mind flew back to her early wedded days, and the man who had stood beside her then, a thrill of tenderness moved her, which if quickened by his living presence might have

become strong. She was young and inexperienced, and had hardly on his late return grown out of the capricious fancies of girlhood.

But he did not come again, and when she thought of his word that he would return once more, if living, and how unlikely he was to break his word, she gave him u]) for dead. So did her parents; so also did another person—that man of silence, of irresistible incisiveness, of still countenance, who was as awake as seven sentinels when he seemed to be as sound asleep as the figures on his family monument. Lord Upland-towers, though not yet thirty, had chuckled like a caustic fogy of threescore when he heard of Barbara's terror and flight at her husband's return, and of the latter's prompt departure. He felt pretty sure, however, that Willowes, despite his hurt feelings, would have reappeared to claim his bright-eyed property if he had been alive at the end of the twelve months.

As there was no husband to live with her, Barbara had relinquished the house prepared for them by her father, and taken up her abode anew at Chene Manor, as in the days of her girlhood. By degrees the episode with Edmond Willowes seemed but a fevered dream, and as the months grew to years Lord Uplandtowers' friendship with the people at Chene—which had somewhat cooled after Barbara's elopement—revived considerably, and he again became a frequent visitor there. He could not make the most trivial alteration or improvement at Knollingwood Hall, where lie lived, without riding off to consult with his friend Sir John at Chene; and thus putting himself frequently under her eyes, Barbara grew accustomed to him, and talked to him as freely as to a brother. She even began to look up to him as a person of authority, judgment, and prudence ; and though his severity on the bench towards poachers, smugglers, and turnip-stealers was matter of common notoriety, she trusted that much of what was said might be misrepresentation.

Thus they lived on till her husband's absence had stretched to years, and there could be no longer any doubt of his death. A passionless manner of renewing his addresses seemed no longer out of place in Lord Uplandtowers. Barbara did not love him, but hers was essentially one of those sweet-pea or with-wind natures, which require a twig of stouter fibre than its own to hang upon and bloom. Now, too, she was older, and admitted to herself that a man whose ancestor had run scores of Saracens through and through in fighting for the site of the Holy Sepulchre was a more desirable husband, socially considered, than one who could only claim with certainty to know that his father and grandfather were respectable burgesses.

Sir John took occasion to inform her that she might legally consider herself a widow; and, in brief. Lord Uplandtowers carried his point with her, and she married him, though he could never get her to own that she loved him as she had loved Willowes. In my childhood I knew an old lady whose mother saw the wedding, and she said that when Lord and Lady Uplandtowers drove away from her father's house in the evening it was in a coach-and-four, and that my lady was dressed in green and silver, and wore the gayest hat and feather that ever were seen—though whether it was that the green did not suit her complexion, or otherwise, the Countess looked pale and the reverse of blooming. After their marriage her husband took her to London, and she saw the gayeties of a season there ; then they returned to Knollingwood Hall, and thus a year passed away.

Before their marriage her husband had seemed to care but little about her inability to love him passionately. "Only let me win you," he had said, "and I will submit to all that." But now her lack of warmth seemed to irritate him, and he conducted himself towards her with a resent-f ulness which led to her passing many hours with him in painful silence. The heir-presumptive to the title was a remote relative, whom Lord Uplandtowers did not exclude from the dislike he entertained towards many persons and things besides, and he had set his mind upon a lineal successor. He blamed her much that there was no promise of this, and asked her what she was good for.

On a particular day in her gloomy life a letter, addressed to her as Mrs. Willowes, reached Lady Uplandtowers from an unexpected quarter. A sculptor in Pisa, knowing nothing of her second marriage, informed her that the long-delayed life-size statue of Mr. Willowes, which, when her husband left that city, he had been directed to retain till it was sent for, was still in his studio. As his commission had not wholly been paid, and the statue was taking up room he could ill spare, he should be very glad to have the debt cleared off, and directions where to forward the figure. Arriving at a time when the Countess was beginning to have little secrets (of a harmless kind, it is true) from lier husband, by reason of their growing estrangement, she replied to this letter without saying a word to Lord Uplandtowers, sending off the balance that was owing to the sculptor, and telling him to despatch the statue to her without delay.

It was some weeks before it arrived at Knollingwood Hall, and, by a singular coincidence, during the interval she received the first absolutely conclusive tidings of her Edmond's death. It had taken place years before, in a foreign land, about six months after their parting, and had been induced by the sufferings he had already undergone, coupled with much depression of spirit, which had caused him to succumb to a slight ailment. The news was sent her in a brief and formal letter from some relative of Willowes's in another part of England.

Her grief took the form of passionate pity for his misfortunes, and of reproach to herself for never having been able to conquer her aversion to his latter image by recollection of what Nature had originally made him. The sad spectacle that had gone from earth had never been her Edmond at all to her. Oh, that she could have met him as he was at first! Thus Barbara thought. It was only a few days later that a wagon with two horses, containing an immense packing-case, was seen at breakfast-time both by Barbara and her husband to drive round to the back of the house, and by-and-by they were informed that a case labelled "Sculpture" had arrived for her ladyship.

"What can that be?" said Lord Upland-towers.

"It is the statue of poor Edmond, which belongs to me, but has never been sent till now," she answered.

"Where are you going to put it?" asked he.

"I have not decided," said the Countess. "Anywhere, so that it will not annoy you."

"Oh, it won't annoy me," says he.

When it had been unpacked in a back room of the house, they went to examine it. The statue was a full-length figure in the purest Carrara marble, representing Edmond Willowes in all his original beauty, as he had stood at parting from her when about to set out on his travels—a specimen of manhood almost perfect in every line and contour. The work had been carried out with absolute fidelity,

"Phoebus-Apollo, sure," said the Earl of Up-landtowers, who had never seen Willowes, real or represented, till now,

Barbara did not hear him. She was standing in a sort of trance before the first husband, as if she had no consciousness of the other husband at her side. The mutilated features of Willowes had disappeared from her mind's eye; this perfect being was really the man she loved, and not that later pitiable figure, in whom love and truth should have seen this image always, but had not done so.

It was not till Lord Uplandtowers said, roughly, "Are you going to stay here all the morning worshipping him?" that she roused herself.

Her husband had not till now the least suspicion that Edmond Willowes originally looked thus, and he thought how deep would have been his jealousy years ago if Willowes had been known to him. Returning to the Hall in the afternoon he found his wife in the gallery, whither the statue had been brought.

She was lost in reverie before it, just as in the morning.

"What are you doing?" he asked.

She started and turned. "I am looking at my husb—my statue, to see if it is well done," she stammered. "Why should I not?"

"There's no reason why," he said. "What are you going to do with the monstrous thing? It can't stand here forever."

"I don't wish it," she said. "I'll find a place."

In her boudoir there was a deep recess, and while the Earl was absent from home for a few days in the following week she hired joiners from the village, who under her directions enclosed the recess with a panelled door. Into the tabernacle thus formed she had the statue placed, fastening the door with a lock, the key of which she kept in her pocket.

When her husband returned he missed the statue from the gallery, and, concluding it had been put away out of deference to his feelings, made no remark. Yet at moments he noticed something on his lady's face which he had never noticed there before. He could not construe it; it was a sort of silent ecstasy, a reserved beatification. What had become of the statue he could not divine, and growing more and more curious, looked about here and there for it till, thinking of her private room, he went towards the spot. After knocking he heard the shutting of a door and the click of a key ; but when he entered, his wife was sitting at work on what was in those days called knotting. Lord Uplandtowers' eye fell upon the newly-painted door where the recess had formerly been.

"You have been carpentering in my absence then, Barbara," he said, carelessly.

"Yes, Uplandtowers."

"Why did you go putting up such a tasteless enclosure as that—spoiling the handsome arch of the alcove?"

"I wanted more closet-room; and I thought that as this was my own apartment—"

" Of course," he returned. Lord Uplandtowers knew now where the statue of young Willowes was.

One night, or rather in the smallest hours of the morning, he missed the Countess from his side. Not being a man of nervous imaginings he fell asleep again before he had much considered the matter, and the next morning had forgotten the incident. But a few nights later the same circumstances occurred. This time he fully roused himself; but before he had moved to search for her, she entered the chamber in her dressing-gown, carrying a candle, which she extinguished as she approached, deeming him asleep. He could discover from her breathino- that she was strangely moved ; but not on this occasion either did he reveal that he had seen her. Presently, when she had laid down, affecting to wake, he asked her some trivial questions. " Yes, Ed-mond,^^ she replied, absently.

Lord Uplandtowers became convinced that she was in the habit of leaving the chamber in this queer way more frequently than he had observed, and he determined to watch. The next midnight he feigned deep sleep, and shortly after perceived her stealthily rise and let herself out of the room

in the dark. He slipped on some clothing and followed. At the farther end of the corridor, where the clash of flint and steel would be out of the hearing of one in the bed-chamber, she struck a light. He stepped aside into an empty room till she had lit a taper and had passed on to her boudoir. In a minute or two he followed. Arrived at the door of the boudoir, he beheld the door of the private recess open, and Barbara within it, standing with her arms clasped tightly round the neck of her Edmond, and her mouth on his. The shawl which she had thrown round her night-clothes had slipped from her shoulders, and her long white robe and pale face lent her the blanched appearance of a second statue embracing the first. Between her kisses, she apostrophized it in a low murmur of infantine tenderness :

"My only love — how could I be so cruel to you, my perfect one — so good and true — I am ever faithful to you, despite my seeming infidelity ! I always think of you—dream of you—during the long hours of the day and in the night-watches ! Oh, Edmond, I am always yours !"

Such words as these, intermingled with sobs, and streaming tears, and dishevelled hair, testified to an intensity of feeling in his wife which Lord Uplandtowers had not dreamed of her possessing.

"Ha, ha!" says he to himself. "This is where we evaj^orate—this is where ray hopes of a successor in the title dissolve—ha, ha! This must be seen to, verily!"

Lord Uplandtowcrs was a subtle man when once he set himself to strategy, though in the present instance he never thought of the simple stratagem of constant tenderness. Nor did he enter the room and surprise his wife as a blunderer would have done, but went back to his chamber as silently as he had left it. When the Countess returned thither, shaken by spent sobs and sighs, he appeared to be soundly sleeping as usual. The next day he began his countermoves by making inquiries as to the whereabouts of the tutor who had travelled with his wife's first husband; this gentleman, he found, was now master of a grammar-school at no great distance from Knollingwood. At the first convenient moment Lord Uplandtowcrs went thither and obtained an interview with the said gentleman. The school-master was much gratified by a visit from such an influential neighbor, and was ready to communicate anything that his lordship desired to know.

After some general conversation on the school and its progress, the visitor observed that he believed the school-master had once travelled a good deal with the unfortunate Mr. Willowes, and had been with him on the occasion of his accident, lie. Lord Ui)landtowers, was interested in knowing what had really happened at that time, and had often thought of inquiring. And then the Earl not only hoard by word of mouth as much as he wished to know, but, their chat

becoming more intimate, the school-master drew upon paper a sketch of the disfigured head, explaining, with bated breath, the various details in the representation.

"It was very strange and terrible!" said Lord Uplandtowers, taking the sketch in his hand. "Neither nose nor ears!"

A poor man in the town nearest to Knolling-wood Hall, who combined the ai't of sign-painting with ingenious mechanical occupations, was sent for by Lord Uplandtowers to come to the Hall on a day in that week when the Countess had gone on a short visit to her parents. His employer made the man understand that the business in which his assistance was demanded was to be considered private, and money insured the observance of this request. The lock of the cupboard was picked, and the ingenious mechanic and painter, assisted by the school-master's sketch, which Lord Uplandtowers had put in his pocket, set to work upon the godlike countenance of the statue under my lord's direction. What the fire had maimed in the original the chisel maimed in the copy. It was a fiendish disfigurement, ruthlessly carried out, and was rendered still more shocking by being tinted to the hues of life, as life had been after the wreck.

Six hours after, when the workman was gone, Lord Uplandtowers looked upon the result, and smiled grimly, and said:

"A statue should represent a man as he appear-
ed in life, and that's as he appeared. Ha! ha! But 'tis done to good purpose, and not idly."

He locked the door of the closet with a skeleton-key, and went his way to fetch the Countess home.

That night she slept, but he kept awake. According to the tale, she murmured soft words in her dream; and he knew that the tender converse of her imaginings was held with one whom he had supplanted but in name. At the end of her dream the Countess of Uplandtowers awoke and arose, and then the enactment of former uierhts was repeated. Her husband remained still and listened. Two strokes sounded from the clock in the pediment without, when, leaving the chamber door ajar, she passed along the corridor to the other end, where, as usual, she obtained a light. So deep was the silence tliat he could even from his bed hear her softly blowing the tinder to a glow after striking the steel. She moved on into the boudoir, and he heard, or fancied he heard, the turning of the key in the closet door. The next moment there came from that direction a loud and prolonged shriek, wliich resounded to the farthest corners of the house. It was repeated, and there was the noise of a heavy fall.

Lord Uplandtowers sprang out of bed. He hastened along the dark corridor to the door of the boudoir, which stood ajar, and, by the light of the candle within, saw his poor young countess lying in a heap in her niglit-dress on the

floor of the closet. When he reached her side he found that she had fainted, much to the relief of his fears that matters were worse. He quickly shut up and locked in the hated image which had done the mischief, and lifted his wife in his arms, where in a few instants she opened her eyes. Pressing her face to his without saying a word, he carried her back to her room, endeavoring as he went to disperse her terrors by a laugh in her ear, oddly compounded of causticity, predilection, and brutality.

"Ho — ho—ho!" says he, "Frightened, dear one, hey ? What a baby 'tis! Only a joke, sure, Barbara—a splendid joke ! But a baby should not go to closets at midnight to look for the ghost of the dear departed! If it do it must expect to be terrified at his aspect—ho—ho—ho !"

When she was in her bed-chamber, and had quite come to herself, though her nerves were still much shaken, he spoke to her more sternly. " Now, my lady, answer me ; do you love him—eh ?"

" No—no !" she faltered, shuddering, with her expanded eyes fixed on her husband. " He is too terrible—no, no!"

" You are sure ?"

"Quite sure!" replied the poor broken-spirited Countess.

But her natural elasticity asserted itself. Next morning he again inquired of her: " Do you love him now?" She quailed under his gaze, but did not reply.

" That means that you do still, by G—!" he continued.

" It means that I will not tell an untruth, and do not wish to incense my lord," she answered, with dignity.

" Then suppose we go and have another look at him?" As he spoke, he suddenly took her by the wrist, and turned as if to lead her towards the ghastly closet.

" No—no ! Oh—no!" she cried, and her desperate wriggle out of his hand revealed that the fright of the night had left more impression upon her delicate soul than superficially appeared.

" Another dose or two, and she will be cured," he said to himself.

It was now so generally known that the Earl and Countess were not in accord, that he took no great trouble to disguise his deeds in relation to this matter. During the daj^ he ordered four men with ropes and rollers to attend him in the boudoir. When they arrived, the closet was open, and the upper part of the statue tied up in canvas. He had it taken to the sleeping-chamber. What followed is more or less matter of conjecture. The story, as told to me, goes on to say that, when Latly Uplandtowers retired with him that night, she saw near the foot of the heavy oak four-poster a tall, dark wardrobe which had not stood there befox'e ; but she did not ask what its presence meant. 8

"I have bad a little whim," he explained, when they were in the dark.

" Have you ?" says she.

" To erect a little shrine, as it may be called."

" A little shrine ?"

" Yes ; to one whom we both equally adore— eh? I'll show you what it contains."

He pulled a cord which hung covered by the bed-curtains, and the doors of the wardrobe slowly opened, disclosing that the shelves within had been removed throughout, and the interior adapted to receive the ghastly figure, which stood there as it had stood in the boudoir, but with a wax-candle burning on each side of it to throw the cropped and distorted features into relief. She clutched him, uttered a low scream, and buried her head in the bedclothes. " Oh, take it away— please take it away!" she implored.

"All in good time ; namely, when you love me best," he returned, calmly. " You don't quite yet —eh?"

"I don't know — I think — oh, Uplandtowers, have mercy—I cannot bear it—oh, in pity, take it away!"

" Nonsense; one gets accustomed to anything. Take another gaze."

In short, he allowed the doors to remain unclosed at the foot of the bed, and the wax-tapers burning; and such was the strange fascination of the grisly exhibition that a morbid curiosity took possession of the Countess as she lay, and, at his

repeated request, she did again look out from the coverlet, shuddered, hid her eyes, and looked again, all the while begging him to take it away, or it would drive her out of her senses. But he would not do so as yet, and the wardrobe was not locked till dawn.

The scene was repeated the next night. Firm in enforcing his ferocious correctives, he continued the treatment till the nerves of the poor lady were quivering in agony under the virtuous tortures inflicted by her lord, to bring her truant heart back to faithfulness.

The third night, when the scene had opened as usual, and she lay staring with immense wild eyes at the horrid fascination, on a sudden she gave an unnatural laugh; she laughed more and more, staring at the image, till she literally shrieked with laughter; then there was silence, and he found her to have become insensible. He thought she had fainted, but soon saw that the event was worse ; she was in an epileptic fit. He started up, dismayed by the sense that, like many other subtle personages, he had been too exacting for his own interests. Such love as he was capable of, though rather a selfish gloating than a cherishing solicitude, was fanned into life on the instant. He closed the wardrobe with the pulley, clasped her in his arms, took her gently to the window, and did all he could to restore her.

It was a long time before the Countess came to herself, and when she did so a considerable change

seemed to have taken place in her emotions. She flung her arms around him, and with gasps of fear abjectly kissed him many times, at last bursting into tears. She had never wept in this scene before.

" You'll take it away, dearest—you will!" she begged, plaintively.

" If you love me."

"I do—oh,I do!"

"And hate him and his memory?"

"Yes—yes!"

"Thoroughly?"

"I cannot endure recollection of him!" cried the poor Countess, slavishly. "It fills me with shame—how could I ever be so depraved! I'll never behave badly again, Uplandtowers; and you will never put the hated statue again before my eyes?"

He felt that he could promise with perfect safety. "Never," said he.

"And then I'll love you," she returned, eagerly, as if dreading lest the scourge should be applied anew. "And I'll never, never dream of thinking a single thought that seems like faithlessness to my marriage vow."

The strange thing now was that this fictitious love wrung from her by terror took on, through mere habit of enactment, a certain quality of reality. A servile mood of attachment to the Earl became distinctly visible in her contemporaneously with an actual dislike for her late husband's mem-cry. This mood of attachment grew and continued when the statue was removed. A permanent revulsion was operant in her, which intensified as time wore on. How fright could have effected such a change of idiosyncrasy learned physicians alone can say; but I believe such cases of reactionary instinct are not unknown.

The upshot was that the cure became so permanent as to be itself a new disease. She clung to hira so tightly that she would not willingly be out of his sight for a moment. She would have no sitting-room apart from his, though she could not help starting when he entered suddenly to her. Her eyes were wellnigh always fixed upon him. If he drove out, she wished to go with him; his slightest civilities to other women made her frantically jealous; till at length her very fidelity became a burden to him, absorbing his time, and curtailing his liberty, and causing him to curse and swear. If he ever spoke sharply to her now, she did not revenge herself by flying off to a mental world of her own; all that affection for another, which had provided her with a resource, was now a cold, black cinder.

From that time the life of this scared and enervated lady—whose existence might have been developed to so much higher purpose but for the ignoble ambition of her parents and the conventions of the time—was one of obsequious amative-ness towards a perverse and cruel man. Little personal events came to her in quick succession—half I a dozen, eight, nine, ten such events; in brief, she bore him no less than eleven children in the eight following years, but half of them came prematurely into the world, or died a few days old; only one, a girl, attained to maturity; she in after-years became the wife of the Honorable Mr. Bel-tonleigh, who was created Lord D'Almaine, as may be remembered.

There was no living son and heir. At length, completely worn out in mind and body. Lady Up-landtowers was taken abroad by her husband, to try the effect of a more genial climate upon her wasted frame. But nothing availed to strengthen her, and she died at Florence a few months after her arrival in Italy.

Contrary to expectation, the Earl of Upland-towers did not marry again. Such affection as existed in him—strange, hard, brutal as it was— seemed untransferable, and the title, as is known, passed at his death to his nephew. Perhaps it may not be so generally known that, during the enlargement of the Hall for the sixth earl, while digging in the grounds for the new foundations, the broken fragments of a marble statue were unearthed. They were submitted to various antiquaries, who said that, so far as the damaged pieces would allow them to form an opinion, the statue seemed to be that of a mutilated Roman satyr, or, if not, an allegorical figure of Death. Only one or two old inhabitants guessed whose statue those fragments had composed.

I should have added that, shortly after the death of the Countess, an excellent sermon was preached by the Dean of Melchester, the subject of which, though names were not mentioned, was unquestionably suggested by the aforesaid events. He dwelt upon the folly of indulgence in sensuous love for a handsome form merely ; and showed that the only rational and virtuous growths of that affection were those based upon intrinsic worth. In the case of the tender but somewhat shallow lady whose life I have related, there is no doubt that an infatuation for the person of young Willowes was the chief feeling that induced her to marry him; which was the more deplorable in that his beauty, by all tradition, was the least of his recommendations, every report bearing out the inference that he must have been a man of steadfast nature, bright intelligence, and promising life.

The company thanked the old surgeon for his story, which the rural dean declared to be a far more striking one than anything he could hope to tell. An elderly member of the Club, who was mostly called the Bookworm, said that a woman's natural instinct of fidelity would, indeed, send back her heart to a man after his death in a truly wonderful manner sometimes — if anything occurred to put before her forcibly the original affection between them, and his original aspect in her eyes—whatever his inferiority may have been, social or otherwise ; and then a general conversation ensued upon the power that a woman has of seeing the actual in the representation, the reality in the dream—a power which (according to the sentimental member) men have no faculty of equalling.

The rural dean thought that such cases as that related by the surgeon were rather an illustration of passion electrified back to life than of a latent, true affection. The story had suggested that he should try to recount to them one which he had used to hear in his youth, and which afforded an instance of the latter and better kind of feeling, his heroine being also a lady who had married beneath her, though he feared his narrative would be of a much slighter kind than the surgeon's. The Club begged him to proceed, and the parson began.

DAME THE THIRD.
Ube /iDarcbioncss of Stonebeiioe*
BY THE RURAL DEAN.

I WOULD have you know, then, that a great many years ago there lived in a dassical mansion with which I used to be familiar, standing not a hundred miles from the city of Melchester, a lady whose personal charms were so rare and unparalleled that she was courted, flattered, and si)oilt by almost all the young noblemen and gentlemen in that part of Wcssex. For a time these attentions pleased her well. But as, in the words of good Robert South (whose sermons might be read much more than they are), the most passionate lover of sport, if tied to follow his hawks and hounds every day of his life, would find the pursuit the greatest torment and calamity, and would fly to the mines and galleys for his recreation, so did this lofty and beautiful lady after a while become satiated with the constant iteration of what she had in its novelty enjoyed; and by an almost natural revulsion turned her regards absolutely netherward, socially speaking. She perversely and passionately centred her affection on quite a plain-looking young man of humble birth and no position at all, though it is true that he was gentle and delicate in nature, of good address, and guileless heart. In short, he was the parish-clerk's son, acting as assistant to the land-steward of her father, the Earl of Avon, with the hope of becoming some day a land-steward himself. It should be said that perhaps the Lady Caroline (as she was called) was a little stimulated in this passion by the discovery that a young girl of the village already loved the young man fondly, and that he had paid some attentions to her, though merely of a casual and good-natured kind.

Since his occupation brought him frequently to the manor-house and its environs. Lady Caroline could make ample opportunities of seeing and speaking to him. She had, in Chaucer's jihrase, "all the craft of fine loving" at her fingers' ends, and the young man, being of a readily-kindling heart, was quick to notice the tenderness in her eyes and voice. He could not at first believe in his good-fortune, having no understanding of her weariness of more artificial men; but a time comes when the stupidest sees in an eye the glance of his other half — and it came to him, who was quite the reverse of dull. As he gained confidence accidental encounters led to encounters by design; till at length, when they were alone together, there was no reserve on the matter. They

whispered tender words as other lovers do, and were as devoted a pair as ever was seen. But not a ray or symptom of this attachment was allowed to show itself to the outer world.

Now, as she became less and less scrupulous towards him under the influence of her affection, and he became more and more reverential under the influence of his, and they looked the situation in the face together, their condition seemed intolerable in its hopelessness. That she could ever ask to be allowed to marry him, or could hold her tongue and quietly renounce him, was equally beyond conception. They resolved upon a third course, possessing neither of the disadvantages of these two—to wed secretly, and live on in outward appearance the same as before. In this they differed from the lovers of my friend's story.

Not a soul in the parental mansion guessea, when Lady Caroline came coolly into the hall one day after a visit to her aunt, that, during tliat visit, her lover and herself had found an opportunity of uniting themselves till death should part them. Yet such was the fact; the young woman who rode fine horses and drove in pony-chaises, and was saluted deferentially by every one, and the young man who trudged about and directed the tree-felling and the laying out of fish-ponds in the park, were husband and wife.

As they had planned, so they acted to the letter for the space of a month and more, clandestinely meeting when and where they best could

do SO ; both being supremely bappy and content. To be sure, towards the latter part of that month, when the first wild warmth of her love bad gone off, the Lady Caroline sometimes wondered within herself how she, who might have chosen a peer of the realm, baronet, knight—or, if serious-minded, a bishop or judge of the more gallant sort who prefer young wives—could have brought herself to do a thing so rash as to make this marriage; particularly when, in their private meetings, she perceived that though her young husband was full of ideas, and fairly well read, they had not a single social experience in common. It was his custom to visit her after nightfall in her own house, when he could find no opportunity for an interview elsewhere ; and to further this course she would contrive to leave unfastened a window on the ground-floor overlooking the lawn, by entering which a back staircase was accessible; so that he could climb up to her apartments, and gain audience of his lady when the house was still.

One dark midnight, when he had not been able to see her during the day, he made use of this secret method, as he had done many times before; and when they had remained in company about an hour he declared that it was time for him to descend.

He would have stayed longer but that the interview had been a somewhat painful one. What she had said to him that night had much excited and angered him, for it had revealed a change in her; cold reason had come to his lofty wife; she was beginning to have more anxiety about her own position and prospects than ardor for him. Whether from the agitation of this perception or not, he was seized with a spasm; he gasped, rose, and in moving towards the window for air he uttered, in a short, thick whisper, "Oh, my heart!"

With his hand upon his chest he sank down to the floor before he had gone another step. By the time that she had relighted the candle, which had been extinguished in case any eye in the opposite grounds should witness his egress, she found that his poor heart had ceased to beat, and there rushed upon her mind what his cottage-friends had once told her, that he was liable to attacks of heart-disease, one of which, the doctor had informed them, might some day carry him off.

Accustomed as she was to doctoring the other parishioners, nothing that she could effect upon him in that kind made any difference whatever; and his stillness, and the increasing coldness of his feet and hands, disclosed too surely to the affrighted young woman that, her husband was dead indeed. For more than an hour, however, she did not abandon her efforts to restore him; when she fully realized the fact that he was a corpse she bent over his body, distracted and bewildered as to what step she next should take.

Her first feelings had undoubtedly been those of passionate grief at the loss of him; her second thoughts were concern at her own position as the daughter of an earl. "Oh, wliy, why, my unfortunate husband, did you die in my chamber at this hour!" she said, piteously, to the corpse. "Why not have died in your own cottage if you would die! Then nobody would ever have known of our imprudent union, and no syllable would have been breathed of how I mismated myself for love of you!"

The clock in the court-yard striking the hour of one aroused Lady Caroline from the stupor into which she had fallen, and she stood up and went towards the door. To awaken and tell her mother seemed her only way out of this terrible situation; yet when she put her hand on the key to unlock it she withdrew herself again. It would be impossible to call even her mother's assistance without risking a revelation to all the world tjirough the servants, while if she could remove the body unassisted to a distance she might avert suspicion of their union even now. This thought of immunity from the social consequences of her rash act, of renewed freedom, was indubitably a relief to her, for, as has b^en said, the constraint and riskiness of her position had begun to tell upon the Lady Caroline's nerves.

She braced herself for the effort, and hastily dressed herself, and then dressed him. Tying his dead hands together with a handkerchief, she laid his arms round her shoulders, and bore him to the landing and down the narrow stairs. Reaching the bottom by the window, she let his body slide slowly over the sill till it lay on the ground without. She then climbed over the window-sill herself, and, leaving the sash open, dragged him on to the lawn with a rustle not louder than the rustle of a broom. There she took a securer hold, and plunged with him under the trees.

Away from the precincts of the house she could apply herself more vigorously to her task, which was a heavy one enough for her, robust as she was; and the exertion and fright she had already undergone began to tell upon her by the time she reached the corner of a beech-plantation which intervened between the Manor-house and the village. Here she was so nearly exhausted that she feared she might have to leave him on the spot, lint she plodded on after a while, and keeping upon the grass at every opportunity she stood at last opposite the poor young man's garden-gate, where he lived with his father, the parish-clerk. How she accomplished the end of her task Lady Caroline never quite knew; but, to avoid leaving traces in the road, she carried him bodily across the gravel, and laid him down at the door. Perfectly aware of his ways of coming and going, she searched behind the shutter for the cottasre door-key, which she placed in his cold hand. Then she kissed his face for the last time, and with silent little sobs bade him farewell.

Lady Caroline retraced her steps, and reached the mansion without hinderance, and to her great relief found the window open just as she had left it. When she had climbed in she listened attentively, fastened the window behind her, and ascending the stairs noiselessly to her room, set everything in order, and returned to bed.

The next morning it was speedily echoed around that the amiable and gentle young villager had been found dead outside his father's door, which he had apparently been in the act of unlocking when he fell. The circumstances were sufficiently exceptional to justify an inquest, at which syncope from heart-disease was ascertained to be beyond doubt the explanation of his death, and no more was said about the matter then. But after the funeral it was rumored that some man who had been returning late from a distant horse-fair had seen, in the gloom of night, a person, apparently a woman, dragging a heavy body of some sort towards the cottage-gate, which, by the light of after-events, would seem to have been the corpse of the young fellow. His clothes were thereupon examined more particularly than at first, with the result that marks of friction were visible upon them here and there, precisely resembling such as would be left by dragging on the ground.

Our beautiful and ingenious Lady Caroline was now in great consternation, and began to think that, after all, it might have been better to honestly confess the truth. But having reached this stage without discovery or suspicion, she determined to make another effort towards concealment; and a bright idea struck her as a means of securing it. I think I mentioned that before she cast eyes on the unfortunate steward's clerk he had been the beloved of a certain village damsel, the woodman's daughter, his neighbor, to whom he had paid some attentions; and possibly he was beloved of her still. At any rate, the Lady Caroline's influence on the estates of her father being considerable, she resolved to seek an interview with the young girl, in furtherance of her plan to save her reputation, about which she was now exceedingly anxious; for by this time, the fit being over, she began to be ashamed of her mad passion for her late husband, and almost wished she had never seen him.

In the course of her parish visiting she lighted on the young girl without much difficulty, and found her looking pale and sad, and wearing a simple black gown, which she had put on out of respect for the young man's memory, whom she had tenderly loved, though he had not loved her.

"Ah, you have lost your lover, Mill\'7d^" said Lady Caroline.

The young woman could not repress her tears. " My lady, he was not quite my lover," she said. " But I was his—and now he is dead I don't care to live any more!"

" Can you keep a secret about him ?" asks the lady—"one in which his honor is involved, which is known to me alone, but should be known to you ?"

0

The girl readily promised, and, indeed, could be safely trusted on such a subject, so deep was her affection for the youth she mourned.

"Then meet me at his grave to-night, half an hour after sunset, and I will tell it to you," says the other.

In the dusk of that spring evening the two shadowy figures of the young women converged upon the assistant steward's newly-turfed mound ; and at that solemn place and hour the one of birth and beauty unfolded her tale : how she had loved him and married him secretly; how he had died in her chamber ; and how, to keep her secret, she had dragged him to his own door.

"Married him, my lady !" said the rustic maiden, starting back.

"I have said so," replied Lady Caroline. "But it was a mad thing, and a mistaken course. He ought to have married you. You, Milly, were peculiarly his. But you lost him."

"Yes," said the poor girl; "and for that they laughed at me. 'Ha, ha! you mid love him, Milly,' they said, 'but he will not love you.'"

"Victory over such unkind jeerers would be sweet," said Lady Caroline. "You lost him in life, but you may have him in death as if you had had him in life, and so turn the tables upon them."

"How ?" said the breathless girl.

The young lady then unfolded her plan, which was that Milly should go forward and declare

that the young man had contracted a secret marriage (as he truly had done) ; that it was with her, Milly, his sweetheart; that he had been visiting her in her cottage on the evening of his death ; when, on finding he was a corpse, she had carried him to his house to prevent discover^'- by her parents, and that she had meant to keep the whole matter a secret, till the rumors afloat had forced it from her.

"And how shall I prove this?" said the woodman's daughter, amazed at the boldness of the proposal.

"Quite sufficiently. You can say, if necessary, that you were married to him at the church of St. Michael, in Bath City, in my name, as the first that occurred to you, to escape detection. That was where he married me. I will support you in this."

"Oh—I don't quite like—"

"If you will do so," said the lady, peremptorily, "I will always be your father's friend and yours; if not, it will be otherwise. And I will give you my wedding-ring, which you shall wear as yours."

"Have you worn it, my lady ?"

"Only at night."

There was not much choice in the matter, and Milly consented. Then this noble lady took from her bosom the ring she had never been able openly to exhibit, and grasping the young girl's hand, slipped it upon her finger as she stood upon her lover's grave.

Milly shivered, and bowed her head, saying, "I feel as if I had become a corpse's bride !"

But from that moment the maiden was heart and soul in the substitution. A blissful repose came over her spirit. It seemed to her that she had secured in death him whom in life she had vainly idolized; and she was almost content. After that the lady handed over to the young man's new wife all the little mementos and trinkets he had given herself, even to a locket containing his hair.

The next day the girl made her so-called confession, which the simple mourning she had already woi'n, without stating for whom, seemed to bear out; and soon the story of the little romance spread through the village and country-side, almost as far as Melchester. It was a curious psychological fact that, having once made the avowal, Milly seemed possessed with a spirit of ecstasy at her position. With the liberal sum of money supplied to her by Lady Caroline she now purchased the garb of a widow, and duly appeared at church in her weeds, her simple face looking so sweet against its margin of crape that she was almost envied her state by the other village girls of her age. And when a woman's sorrow for her beloved can maim her young life so obviously as it had done Milly's there was, in truth, little subterfuge in the case. Her explanation tallied so well with the details of her lover's latter movements—those strange absences and sudden return-

ings which had occasionally puzzled his friends —that nobody supposed for a moment that the second actor in these secret nuptials was other than she. The actual and whole trutii would, indeed, have seemed a preposterous assertion beside this plausible one, by reason of the lofty demeanor of the Lady Caroline and the unassuming habits of the late villager. There being no inheritance in question, not a soul took the trouble to go to the city church, forty miles off, and search the registers for marriage signatures bearing out so humble a romance.

In a short time Milly caused a decent tombstone to be erected over her nominal husband's grave, whereon appeared the statement that it was placed there by his heart-broken widow,w]uch,considering that the payment for it came from Lady Caroline and the grief from Milly, was as truthful as such inscriptions usually are, and only required pluralizing to render it yet more nearly so.

The impressionable and complaisant Milly, in her character of widow, took delight in going to his grave every day, and indulging in sorrow which was a positive luxury to her. She placed fresh flowers on his grave, and so keen was her emotional imaginativeness that she almost believed herself to have been his wife indeed as she walked to and fro in her garb of woe. One afternoon, Milly being busily engaged in this labor of love at the grave, Lady Caroline passed outside the church-yard wall with some of her visiting

friends, who, seeing Milly there, watched her actions with interest, remarked upon the pathos of the scene, and upon the intense affection the young man must have felt for such a tender creature as Milly. A strange light, as of pain, shot from the Lady Caroline's eye, as if for the first time she begrudged to the young girl the position she had been at such pains to transfer to her; it showed that a slumbering affection for her husband still had life in Lady Caroline, obscured and stifled as it was by social considerations.

An end was put to this smooth arrangement by the sudden appearance in the church-yard one day of the Lady Caroline, when Milly had come there on her usual errand of laying flowers. Lady Caroline had been anxiously awaiting her behind the chancel, and her countenance was pale and agitated.

" Milly," she said, " come here ! I don't know how to say to you what I am going to say. I am half dead!"

"I am sorry for your ladyship," says Milly, wondering.

" Give me that ring !" says the lady, snatching at the girl's left hand.

Milly drew it quickly away.

" I tell you, give it to me!" repeated Lady Caroline, almost fiercely. " Oh—but you don't know why! I am in a grief and a trouble I did not expect !" And Lady Caroline whispered a few words to the girl.

" Oh, my lady !" said tlie thunderstruck Milly. " What will you do ?"

"You must say that your statement was a wicked lie, an invention, a scandal, a deadly sin —that I told you to make it to screen me! That it was I whom he married at Bath. In short, we must tell the truth, or I am ruined—body, mind, and reputation—forever!"

But there is a limit to the flexibility of gentle-souled women, Milly by this time had so grown to the idea of being one flesh with this young man, of having the right to bear his name as she bore it; had so thoroughly come to regard him as her husband, to dream of him as her husband, to speak of him as her husband, that she could not relinquish him at a moment's perem^jtory notice.

"No, no," she said, desperately, "I cannot—I will not—give him up ! Your ladyship took him away from me alive, and gave him back to me only when he was dead. Now I will keep him ! I am truly his widow. More truly than you, my lady, for I love him and mourn for him, and call myself by his dear name, and your ladyship does neither !"

" I do love him !" cries Lady Caroline, with flashing eyes, "and I cling to him, and won't let him go to such as you ! How can I, when he is tlu' father of this poor babe that's coming to me ? I must have him back again ! Milly, Milly, can't you pity and understand me, perverse girl that you are, and the miserable plight that I am in? Oh, this precipitancy—it is the ruin of women ! Why did I not consider, and wait! Come, give me back all that I have given you, and assure me you will support me in confessing the truth !"

" Never, never !" persisted Milly, with woe-be-gone passionateness. " Look at this headstone ! Look at my gown and bonnet of crape—this ring : listen to the name they call me by! My character is worth as much to me as yours is to you ! After declaring my love mine, myself his, taking his name, making his death my own particular sorrow, how can I say it was not so ? No such dishonor for me ! I will outswear you, my lady ; and I shall be believed. My story is so much the more likely that yours will be thought false. But, oh please, my lady, do not drive me to this ! In pity, let me keep him !"

The poor nominal widow exhibited such anguish at a proposal which would have been truly a bitter humiliation to her, that Lady Caroline was warmed to pity in spite of her own condition.

" Yes, I see your position," she answered. " But think of mine ! What can I do ? Without your support it would seem an invention to save me from disgrace; even if I produced the register, the love of scandal in the world is such that the multitude would slur over the fact, say it was a fabrication, and believe your story. I do not know who were the witnesses, or anything !"

In a few minutes these two poor young women felt, as 80 many in a strait have felt before, that union was their greatest strength, even now ; and they consulted calmly together. The result of their deliberations was that Milly went home as usual, and Lady Caroline also, the latter confessing that very night to the Countess, her mother, of the marriage, and to nobody else in the world. And, some time after. Lady Caroline and her mother went away to London, where a little while later still they were joined by Milly, who was supposed to have left the village to proceed to a watering-place in the North for the benefit of her health, at the expense of the ladies of the Manor, who had been much interested in her state of lonely and defenceless widowhood.

Early the next year the widow Milly came home with an infant in her arms, the family at the Manor-house having meanwhile gone abroad. They did not return from their tour till the autumn ensuing, by which time Milly and the child had again departed from the cottage of her father the woodman, Milly having attained to the dignity of dwelling in a cottage of her own, many miles to the eastward of lier native village ; a comfortable little allowance had, moreover, been settled on her and the child for life, through the instrumentality of Lady Caroline and her mother.

Two or three years passed away, and the Lady Caroline married a nobleman — the Marquis of Stonehenge — considerably her senior, who had wooed her long and phlegmatically. He was not rich, but she led a placid life with him for many years, though there was no child of the marriage. Meanwhile Milly's boy, as the youngster was called, and as Milly herself considered him, grew up and throve wonderfully, and loved her as she deserved to be loved for her devotion to him, in whom she every day traced more distinctly the lineaments of the man who had won her girlish heart, and kept it even in the tomb.

She educated him as well as she could with the limited means at her disposal, for the allowance had never been increased. Lady Caroline, or the Marchioness of Stonehenge as she now was, seeming by degrees to care little what had become of them. Milly became extremely ambitious on the boy's account; she pinched herself almost of necessaries to send him to the grammar-school in the town to which they retired, and at twenty he enlisted in a cavalry regiment, joining it with a deliberate intent of making the army his profession and not in a freak of idleness. His exceptional attainments, his manly bearing, his steady conduct, speedily won him promotion, which was furthered by the serious war in which his country was at that time engaged. On his return to England after the peace he had risen to the rank of riding-master, and was soon after advanced another stage, and made quartermaster, though still a young man.

His mother—his corporeal mother, that is, the Marchioness of Stonehenge—heard tidings of this unaided progress; it reawakened her maternal instincts and filled her with pride. She became keenly interested in her successful soldier-son; and as she grew older much wished to see him again, particularly when, the Marquis dying, she was left a solitary and childless widow. Whether or not she would have gone to him of her own impulse I cannot say; but one day, when she was driving in an open carriage in the outskirts of a neighboring town, the troops lying at the barracks hard by passed her in marching order. She eyed them narrowly, and in the finest of the horsemen recognized her son from his likeness to her first husband.

This sight of him doubly intensified the motherly emotions which had lain dormant in her for so many years, and she wildly asked herself how she could so have neglected him. Had she possessed the true courage of affection she would have owned to her first marriage, and have reared him as her son! What would it have mattered if she had never obtained this precious coronet of pearls and gold leaves, by comparison with the gain of having the love and protection of such a noble and worthy son? These and other sad reflections cut the gloomy and solitary lady to the heart, and she repented of her pride in disclaiming her first husband more bitterly than she had ever repented of her infatuation in marrying him.

Her yearning was so strong that at length it seemed to her that she could not live without announcing herself to him as his mother. Come what might, she would do it; late as it was, she would have him away from that woman whom she began to hate with the fierceness of a deserted heart, for having taken her place as the mother of her only child. She felt confidently enough that her son would only too gladly exchange a cottage mother for one who was a peeress of the realm. Being now, in her widowhood, free to come and go as she chose without question from anybody, Lady Stonehenge started next day for the little town where Milly yet lived, still in her robes of sable for the lost lover of her youth.

"He is my son," said the Marchioness, as soon as she was alone in the cottage with Milly. "You must give him back to me, now that I am in a position in which I can defy the world's opinion. I suppose he comes to see you continually?"

"Every month since he returned from the war, ray lady. And sometimes he stays two or three days, and takes me about seeing sights everywhere!" She spoke with quiet triumph.

"Well, you will have to give him up," said the Marchioness, calmly. "It shall not be the worse for you—you may see him when you choose. I am going to avow my first marriage and have him with me."

"You forget that there are two to be reckoned with, my lady. Not only me, but himself."

"That can be arranged. You don't suppose that he wouldn't—" But not wishing to insult Milly by comparing their positions, she said, "He is my own flesh and blood, not yours."

"Flesh and blood's nothing!" said Milly, flashing with as much scorn as a cottager could show to a peeress, which, in this case, was not so little as may be supposed. "But I will agree to put it to him, and let him settle it for himself."

"That's all I require," said Lady Stonehenge. "You must ask him to come, and I will meet him here."

The soldier was written to, and the meeting took place. He was not so much astonished at the disclosure of his parentage as Lady Stonehenge had been led to expect, having known for years that there was a little mystery al)Out his birth. His manner towards the Marchioness, though respectful, was less warm than she could have hoped. The alternatives as to his choice of a mother were put before him. His answer amazed and stupefied her.

"No, my lady," he said. "Thank you much, but I prefer to let things be as they have been. My father's name is mine, in any case. You see, my lady, you cared little for me when I was weak and helpless. Why should I come to you now I am strong? She—dear, devoted soul"—pointing to Milly—"tended me from my birth, watched over me, nursed me when I was ill, and deprived herself of many a little comfort to push me on. T cannot love another mother as I love her. She is my mother, and I will always be her son!" As he spoke he put his manly arm around Milly's neck, and kissed her with the tenderest affection.

The agony of the poor Marchioness was pitiable. "You kill me!" she said, between her shaking sobs. "Cannot you—love—me—too?"

"No, my lady. If I must say it, you were ashamed of my poor father, who was a sincere and honest man; therefore, I am ashamed of you."

Nothing would move him; and the suffering woman at last gasped, "Cannot—oh, cannot you give one kiss to me—as you did to her? It is not much—it is all I ask—all!"

"Certainly," he replied.

He kissed her coldly, and the painful scene came to an end. That day was the beginning of death to the unfortunate Marchioness of Stone-henge. It was in the perverseness of her human heart that his denial of her should add fuel to the fire of her craving for his love. How long afterwards she lived I do not know with any exactness, but it was no great length of time. That anguish that is sharper than a serpent's tooth wore her out soon. Utterly reckless of the world, its ways and its opinions, she allowed her story to become known; and when the welcome end supervened (which, I grieve to say, she refused to lighten by the consolations of religion), a broken heart was the truest phrase in which to sum up its cause.

The rural dean having concluded, some observations upon his tale were made in due course. The sentimental member said that Lady Caroline's history afforded a sad instance of how an honest human affection will become shamefaced and mean under the frost of class-division and social prejudices. She probably deserved some pity ; though her offspring, before he grew up to man's estate, had deserved more. There was no pathos like the pathos of childhood, when a child found itself in a world where it was not wanted, and could not understand the reason why. A tale by the speaker, further illustrating the same subject, though with different results from the last, naturally followed.

DAME THE FOURTH.
Xa&^ /IDottisfont
BY THE SENTIMENTAL MEMBER.

Of all the romantic towns in Wessex, Winton-cester is probably tbe most convenient for meditative people to live in, since there you have a cathedral with a nave so long that it affords space in which to walk and summon your remoter moods without continually turning on your heel, or seeming to do more than take an afternoon stroll under cover from the rain or sun. In an uninterrupted course of nearly three hundred steps eastward, and again nearly three hundred steps westward amid those magnificent tombs, you can, for instance, compare in the most leisurely way the dry dustiness which ultimately pervades the persons of kings and bishops with the damper dustiness that is usually the final shape of commoners, curates, and others who take their last rest out of doors. Then, if you are in love, you can, by sauntering in the chapels and behind the Episcopal chantries with the bright-eyed one, so steep

and mellow your ecstasy in the solemnities around, that it will assume a rarer and finer tincture, even more grateful to the understanding, if not to the senses, than that form of the emotion which arises from such companionship in spots where all is life and growth and fecundity.

It was in this solemn place, whither they had withdrawn from the sight of relatives on one cold day in March, that Sir Ashley Mottisfont asked in marriage, as his second wife, Pliilippa, the gentle daughter of plain Squire Okehall. Her life bad been an obscure one thus far, while Sir Ashley, though not a rich man, had a certain distinction about him; so that everybody thought what a convenient, elevating, and, in a word, blessed match it would be for such a supernumerary as she. Nobody thought so more than the amiable girl herself. She had been smitten with such affection for him that, when she walked the cathedral aisles at his side on the before-mentioned day, she did not know that her feet touched hard pavement; it seemed to her rather that she was floating in space. Philippa was an ecstatic, heart-thumping maiden, and could not understand how she had deserved to have sent to her such an illustrious lover, such a travelled personage, such a handsome man.

AVhen he put the question, it was in no clumsy language, such as the ordinary bucolic county landlords were wont to use on like quivering occasions, but as elegantly as if he had been taught 10

it in Enfield's Speaker. Yet he hesitated a little —for he had something to add.

"My pretty Philippa," he said (she was not very pretty, by the way), "I have, you must know, a little girl dependent upon me : a little waif I found one day in a patch of wild oats "— such was this worthy baronet's humor—"when I was riding home : a little nameless creature, whom I wish to take care of till she is old enough to take care of herself, and to educate in a plain way. She is only fifteen months old, and is at present in the hands of a kind villager's wife in my parish. Will you object to give some attention to the little thing in her helplessness?"

It need hardly be said that our innocent young lady, loving him so deeply and joyfully as she did, replied that she would do all she could for the nameless child; and shortly afterwards the pair were married in the same cathedral that had echoed the whispers of his declaration, the officiating minister being the Bishop himself, a venerable and experienced man, so well accomplished in uniting people who had a mind for that sort of experiment, that the couple, with some sense of surprise, found themselves one while they were still vaguely gazing at nach other as two independent beings.

After this operation they went home to Deans-leigh Park, and made a beginning of living happily ever after. Lady Mottisfont, true to her promise, was always running down to the village during the following weeks to see the baby whom her husband had so mysteriously lighted on during his ride home—concerning which interesting discovery she had her own oiDinion ; but being so extremely amiable and affectionate that she could have loved stocks and stones if there had been no living creatures to love, she uttered none of her thoughts. The little thing, who had been christened Dorothy, took to Lady Mottisfont as if the Baronet's young wife had been her mother; and at length Pliilippa grew so fond of the child that she ventured to ask her husband if she might have 'Dorothy in her own home, and bring her up carefully, just as if she were her own. To this be answered that, though remarks might be made thereon, he bad no objection—a fact which was obvious. Sir Ashley seeming rather pleased than otherwise with the proposal.

After this they lived quietly and uneventfully for two or three years at Sir Asliley Mottisfont's residence in that part of England, with as near an approach to bliss as the climate of this country allows. The child had been a godsend to Phi-lippa, for there seemed no great probability of her having one of her own : and she wisely regarded the possession of Dorothy as a special kindness of Providence, and did not worry her mind at all as to Dorothy's possible origin. Being a tender and impulsive creature, she loved her husband without criticism, exhaustively and religiously, and the child not much otherwise. She watched the little foundling as if she had been her own by nature, and Dorothy became a great solace to her when her husband was absent on pleasure or business ; and when he came home he looked pleased to see how the two had won each other's hearts. Sir Ashley would kiss his wife, and his wife would kiss little Dorothy, and little Dorothy would kiss Sir Ashley, and after this triangular burst of affection Lady Mottisfont would say, " Dear me — I forget she is not mine!"

" What does it matter ?" her husband would reply. "Providence is foreknowing. He has sent us this one because He is not intending to send us one by any other channel."

Their life was of the simplest. Since his travels the Baronet had taken to sporting and farming, while Philippa was a pattern of domesticity. Their pleasures were all local. They retired eai'ly to rest, and rose with the cart-horses and whistling wagoners. They knew the names of every bird and tree not exceptionally uncommon, and could foretell the weather almost as well as anxious farmers and old people with corns.

One day Sir Ashley Mottisfont received a letter, which he read and musingly laid down on the table without remark.

" What is it, dearest ?" asked his wife, glancing at the sheet.

" Oh, it is from an old lawyer at Bath whom I used to know. He reminds me of something said to him four or five years ago—some little time before we were married—about Dorothy."

" What about her ?"

" It was a casual remark I made to him, when I thought you might not take kindly to her, that if he knew a lady who was anxious to adopt a child, and could insure a good home to Dorothy, he was to let me know."

"But that was when you had nobody to take care of her," she said, quickly, " How absurd of him to write now! Does he know you are married ? He must, surely."

"Oh yes!"

He handed her the letter. The solicitor stated that a widow lady of position, who did not at present wish her name to be disclosed, had lately become a client of his while taking the waters, and had mentioned to him that she would like a little girl to bring up as her own, if she could be certain of finding one of good and pleasing disposition ; and, the better to insure this, she would not wish the child to be too young for judging her qualities. He had remembered Sir Ashley's observation to him a long while ago, and therefore brought the matter before him. It would be an excellent home for the little girl—of that he was positive —if she had not already found such a home.

"But it is absurd of the man to write so loner after!" said Lady Mottisfont, with a lunipiness about the back of her throat as she thought how much Dorothy had become to her. " I suppose it

was when you first—found her—that you told him this ?"

" Exactly—it was then."

He fell into thought, and neither Sir Ashley nor Lady Mottisfont took the trouble to answer the lawyer's letter j and so the matter ended for the time.

One day at dinner, on their return from a short absence in town, whither they had gone to see what the world was doing, hear what it was saying, and to make themselves generally fashionable after rusticating for so long—on this occasion, I say, they learned from some friend who had joined them at dinner that Fernell Hall—the manorial house of the estate next their own, which had been offered on lease by reason of the impecuniosity of its owner—had been taken for a term by a widow lady, an Italian contessa, whose name I will not mention for certain reasons which may by-and-by appear. Lady Mottisfont expressed her surprise and interest at the probability of having such a neighbor. "Though, if I had been born in Italy, I think I should have liked to remain there," she said.

"She is not Italian, though her husband was," said Sir Ashley.

" Oh, you have heard about her before now?"

" Yes; they were talking of her at Grey's the other evening. She is English." And then, as her husband said no more about the lady, the friend who was dining with them told Lady

Mottisfont that the Countess's father had speculated largely in East India stock, in which immense fortunes were being made at that time; through this his daughter had found herself enormously wealthy at his death, which had occurred only a few weeks after the death of her husband. It was supposed that the marriage of an enterprising English speculator's daughter to a poor foreign nobleman had been matter of arrangement merely. As soon as the Countess's widowhood was a little further advanced she would, no doubt, be the mark of all the schemers who came near her, for she was still quite young. But at present she seemed to desire quiet, and avoided society and town.

Some weeks after this time Sir Ashley Mottisfont sat looking fixedly at his lady for many moments. He said:

" It might have been better for Dorothy if the Countess had taken her. She is so wealthy in comparison with ourselves, and could have ushered the girl into the great world more effectually than we ever shall be able to do."

"The Contessa take Dorothy ?" said Lady Mottisfont, with a start. " What—was she the lady who Avished to adopt her ?"

" Yes; she was staying at Bath when Lawyer Gayton wrote to me."

" But how do you know all this, Ashley ?"

He showed a little hesitation. " Oh, I've seen her," he says. "You know, she drives to the meet sometimes, though she does not ride ; and she has informed me that she was the lady who inquired of Gaytoh."

"You have talked to her as well as seen her, then ?"

" Oh yes, several times ; everybody has."

" Why didn't you tell me ?" says his lady. " I had quite forgotten to call upon her. I'll go tomorrow, or soon, . . . But I can't think, Ashley, how you can say that it might have been better for Dorothy to have gone to her; she is so much our own now that I cannot admit any such conjectures as those, even in jest." Her eyes reproached him so eloquently that Sir Ashley Mottisfont did not answer.

Lady Mottisfont did not hunt any more than the Anglo-Italian Countess did; indeed, she had become so absorbed in household matters and in Dorothy's well - being that she had no mind to waste a minute on mere enjoyments. As she had said, to talk coolly of what might have been the best destination in days past for a child to whom they had become so attached seemed quite barbarous, and she could not understand how her husband should consider the point so abstractedly ; for, as will probably have been guessed, Lady Mottisfont long before this time, if she had not done so at the very beginning, divined Sir Ashley's true relation to Dorothy. But the Baronet's wife was so discreetly meek and mild that she never told him of her surmise, and took what Heaven had sent her without cavil, her generosity in this respect having been bountifully rewarded by the new life she found in her love for the little girl.

Her husband recurred to the same uncomfortable subject when, a few days later, they were speaking of travelling abroad. He said that it was almost a pity, if they thought of going, that they had not fallen in with the Countess's wish. That lady had told him that she had met Dorothy walking with her nurse, and that she had never seen a child she liked so well.

" What—she covets her still ? How impertinent of the woman !" said Lady Mottisfont.

" She seems to do so. . . . You see, dearest Phi-lippa, the advantage to Dorothy would have been that the Countess would have adopted her legally, and have made her as her own daughter; while we have not done that—we are only bringing up and educating a poor child in charity."

" But I'll adopt her fully—make her mine legally !" cried his wife, in an anxious voice. " How is it to be done?"

" H'm." He did not inform her, but fell into thought; and, for reasons of her own, his lady was restless and uneasy.

The very next day Lady Mottisfont drove to Fernell Hall to pay the neglected call upon her neighbor. The Countess was at home, and received her graciously. But poor Lady Mottisfont's heart died within her as soon as sue set eyes on her new acquaintance. Such wonderful beauty, of the fully-developed kind, had never confronted her before inside the lines of a human face. She seemed to shine with every light and grace that woman can possess. Her finished Continental manners, her expanded mind, her ready wit, composed a study that made the other poor lady sick ; for she, and latterly Sir Ashley himself, were rather rural in manners, and she felt abashed by new sounds and ideas from without. She hardly knew three words in any language but her own, while this divine creature, though truly English, had, apparently, whatever she wanted in the Italian and French tongues to suit every impression ; which was considered a great improvement to speech in those days, and, indeed, is by many considered as such in these.

" How very strange it was about the little girl!" the Contessa said to Lady Mottisfont, in her gay tones. " I mean, that the child the lawyer recommended should, just before then, have been adopted by you, who are now my neighbor. How is she getting on ? I must come and see her."

" Do you still want her?" asks Lady Mottisfont, suspiciously.

" Oh, I should like to have her!"

" But you can't! She's mine !" said the other, greedily.

A drooping manner appeared in the Countess from that moment.

Lady Mottisfont, too, was in a wretched mood

all the way home that day. The Countess was so charming in every way that she had charmed her gentle ladyship; how should it be possible that she had failed to charm Sir Ashley? Moreover, she had awakened a strange thought in Phi-lippa's mind. As soon as she reached home she rushed to the nursery, and there, seizing Dorothy, frantically kissed her; then, holding her at arm's-length, she gazed with a piercing inquisitiveness into the girl's lineaments. She sighed deeply, abandoned the wondering Dorothy, and hastened away.

She had seen there not only her husband's traits, which she had often beheld before, but others, of the shade, shape, and expression which characterized those of her new neighbor.

Then this poor lady perceived the whole perturbing sequence of things, and asked herself how she could have been such a walking piece of simplicity as not to have thought of this before. But she did not stay long upbraiding herself for her short-sightedness, so overwhelmed was she with misery at the spectacle of herself as an intruder between these. To be sure she could not have foreseen such a conjuncture; but that did not lessen her grief. The woman who had been both her husband's bliss and his backsliding had reappeared free when he was no longer so, and she evidently was dying to claim her own in the person of Dorothy, who had meanwhile grown to be, to Lady Mottisfont, almost the only source of each

day's happiness, supplying her with something to watch over, inspiring her with the sense of maternity, and so largely reflecting her husband's nature as almost to deceive her into the pleasant belief that she reflected her own also.

If there was a single direction in which this devoted and virtuous lady erred, it was in the direction of over-submissiveness. When all is said and done, and the truth told, men seldom show much self-sacrifice in their conduct as lords and masters to helpless women bound to them for life, and perhaps (though I say it with all uncertainty) if she had blazed up in his face like a furze-fagot, directly he came home, she might have helped herself a little. But God knows whether this is a true supposition; at any rate, she did no such thing; and waited and prayed that she might never do despite to him who, she was bound to admit, had always been tender and courteous towards her; and hoped that little Dorothy might never be taken away.

By degrees the two households became friendly, and very seldom did a week pass without their seeing something of each other. Try as she might, and dangerous as she assumed the acquaintanceship to be. Lady Mottisfont could detect no fault or flaw in her new friend. It was obvious that Dorothy had been the magnet which had drawn the Contessa hither, and not Sir Ashley. Such beauty, united with such understanding and brightness, Philippa had never before known in one of her own sex, and she tried to think (whether she succeeded I do not know) that she did not mind the propinquity ; since a woman so rich, so fair, and with such a command of suitors, could not desire to wreck the happiness of so inoffensive a person as herself.

The season drew on when it was the custom for families of distinction to go off to The Bath, and Sir Ashley Mottisfont persuaded his wife to accompany him thither with Dorothy. Everybody of any note Avas there this year. From their own part of England came many that they kncAV; among the rest, Lord and Lady Purbeck, the Earl and Countess of Wessex, Sir John Grebe, the Drenkhards, Lady Stourvale, the old Duke of Hamptonshire, the Bishop of IVIelchester, the Dean of Exonbury, and other lesser lights of Court, pulpit, and field. Thither also came the fair Contessa, whom, as soon as Philippa saw how much she was sought after by younger men, she could not conscientiously suspect of renewed designs upon Sir Ashley.

But the Countess had finer opportunities than ever with Dorothy ; for Lady Mottisi'unt was often indisposed, and even at other times could not honestly hinder an intercourse which gave bright ideas to the child, Dorothy welcomed her new acquaintance with a strange and instinctive readiness that intimated the wonderful subtlety of the threads which bind flesh and flesh together.

At last the crisis came : it was precipitated by an accident. Dorothy and her nurse had gone out one day for an airing, leaving Lady Mottis-font alone in-doors. While she sat gloomily thinking that in all likelihood the Countess would contrive to meet the child somewhere, and exchange a few tender words with her. Sir Ashley Mottis-font rushed in and informed her that Dorothy had just had the narrowest possible escape from death. Some workmen were undermining a house to pull it down for rebuilding, when, without warning, the front wall inclined slowly outward for its fall, the nurse and child passing beneath it at the same moment. The fall was temporarily arrested by the scaffolding, while in the mean time the Countess had witnessed their imminent danger from the other side of the street. Springing across, she snatched Dorothy from under the wall, and pulled the nurse after her, the middle of the way being barely reached before they were enveloped in the dense dust of the descending mass, though not a stone touched them.

"Where is Dorothy?" says the excited Lady Mottisfont.

" She has her—she won't let her go for a time—"

" Has her? But she's mine —she's mine!" cries Lady Mottisfont.

Then her quick and tender eyes perceived that her husband had almost forgotten her intrusive existence in contemplating the oneness of Dorothy's, the Countess's, and his own; he was in a dream of exaltation which recognized nothing necessary to his well-being outside that welded circle of three lives.

Dorothy was at length brought home ; she was much fascinated by the Countess, and saw nothing tragic, but rather all that was truly delightful, in what had happened. In the evening, when the excitement was over, and Dorothy was put to bed, Sir Ashley said, " She has saved Dorothy; and I have been asking myself what I can do for her as a slight acknowledgment of her heroism. Surely we ought to let her have Dorothy to bring up, since she still desires to do it? It would be so much to Dorothy's advantage. We ought to look at it in that light, and not selfishly."

Philippa seized his hand. "Ashley, Ashley! You don't mean it—that I must lose ray pretty darling—the only one I have?" She met his gaze with her piteous mouth and wet eyes so painfully strained that he turned away his face.

The next morning, before Dorothy was awake, Lady Mottisfont stole to the girl's bedside and sat regarding her. When Dorothy opened her eyes, she fixed them for a long time upon Philip-pa's features.

"Mamma, you are not so pretty as the Con-tesse, are you ?" she said, at length.

"I am not, Dorothy."

" Why are you not, mamma ?"

" Dorothy, where would you rather live, always —with me or with her?"

The little girl looked troubled. "I am sorry, mamma ; I don't mean to be unkind ; but I would rather live with her—I mean, if I might without trouble, and you did not mind, and it could be just the same to us all, you know."

" Has she ever asked you the same question ?"

" Never, mamma."

There lay the sting of it: the Countess seemed the soul of honor and fairness in this matter, test her as she might. That afternoon Lady Mottis-font went to her husband with singular firmness upon her gentle face.

"Ashley, we have been married nearly five years, and I have never challenged you with what I know perfectly well—the parentage of Dorothy."

" Never have you, Philippa dear; though I have seen that you knew from the first."

" From the first as to her father, not as to her mother. Her I did not know for some time ; but I know now."

"Ah, you have discovered that, too?" says he, without much surprise.

" Could I help it? Very well; that being so, I have thought it over, and I have spoken to Dorothy. I agree to her going. I can do no less than grant to the Countess her wish, after her kindness to ray—your—her—child."

Then this self-sacrificing woman went hastily away that he might not see that her heart was bursting; and thereupon, before they left the city, Dorothy changed her mother and her home.

After this, the Countess went away to London for a while, taking Dorothy with her ; and the Baronet and his wife returned to their lonely place at Deansleigh Park without her.

To renounce Dorothy in the bustle of Bath was a different thing from living without her in this quiet home. One evening Sir Ashley missed his wife from the supper-table ; her manner had been 80 pensive and woful of late that he immediately became alarmed. He said nothing, but looked about outside the house narrowly, and discerned her form in the park, where recently she had been accustomed to walk alone. In its lower levels there was a pool fed by a trickling brook, and he reached this spot in time to hear a splash. Running forward, he dimly perceived her light gown floating in the water. To pull her out was the work of a few instants, and bearing her in-doors to her room, he undressed her, nobody in the house knowing of the incident but himself. She had not been immersed long enough to lose her senses, and soon recovered. She owned that she had done it because the Contessa had taken away her child, as she persisted in calling Dorothy. Iler husband spoke sternly to her, and impressed upon her the weakness of giving way thus, when all that had happened was for the best. She took his reproof meekly, and admitted her fault.

After that she became more resigned, but he often caught her in tears over some doll, shoe, or ribbon of Dorothy's, and decided to take her to the North of England for change of air and scene. This was not without its beneficial effect, corporeally no less than mentally, as later events showed, but she still evinced a preternatural sharpness of ear at the most casual mention of the child. When they reached home, the Countess and Dorothy were still absent from the neighboring Fernell Hall, but in a month or two they returned, and a little later Sir Ashley Mottisfont came into his wife's room full of news.

"Well, would you think it, Philippa? After being so desperate, too, about getting Dorothy to be with her!"

"Ah—what?"

"Our neighbor, the Countess, is going to be married again! It is to somebody she has met in London."

Lady Mottisfont was much surprised; she had never dreamed of such an event. The conflict for the possession of Dorothy's person had obscured the possibility of it; yet what more likely, the Countess being still under thirty, and so good-looking?

" What is of still more interest to us, or to you, continued her husband, " is a kind offer she has made. She is willing that you should have Dorothy back again. Seeing what a grief the loss of her has been to you, she will try to do without her."

" It is not for that; it is not to oblige me," said Lady Mottisfont, quickly. "One can see well enough what it is for!"

" Well, never mind ; beggars mustn't be choosers. The reason or motive is nothing to us, so that you obtain your desire."

"I am not a beggar any longer," said Lady Mottisfont, with proud mystery.

" What do you mean by that ?"

Lady Mottisfont hesitated. However, it was only too plain that she did not now jump at a restitution of one for whom some months before she had been breaking her heart.

The explanation of this change of mood became apparent some little time further on. Lady Mottisfont, after five years of wedded life, was expecting to become a mother, and the aspect of many things was greatly altered in her view. Among the more important changes was that of no longer feeling Dorothy to be absolutely indispensable to her existence.

Meanwhile, in view of her coming marriage, the Countess decided to abandon tbe remainder of her term at Fernell Hall, and return to her pretty little house in town. But she could not do this quite so quickly as she had expected, and half a year or more elapsed before she finally quitted the neighborhood, the interval being passed in alternations between the country and London. Prior to her last departure she had an interview with Sir Ashley Mottisfont, and it occurred three days after his wife had presented him with a son and heir.

" I wanted to speak to you," said the Countess, looking him luminously in the face, "about the dear foundling I have adopted temporarily, and thought to have adopted permanently. But my marriage makes it too risky."

" I thought it might be that," he answered, regarding her steadfastly back again, and observing two tears come slowly into her eyes as she heard her own voice describe Dorothy in those words.

" Don't criticise me," she said, hastily; and recovering herself, went on. " If Lady Mottisfont could take her back again, as I suggested, it would be better for me, and certainly no worse for Dorothy. To every one but ourselves she is but a child I have taken a fancy to, and Lady Mottisfont coveted her so much, and was very reluctant to let her go. ... I am sure she will adopt her again?" she added, anxiously.

"I will sound her afresh," said the Baronet. "You leave Dorothy behind for the present?"

"Yes ; although I go away, I do not give up the house for another month."

He did not speak to his wife about the proposal till some few days after, when Lady Mottisfont had nearly recovered, and news of the Countess's marriage in London had just reached them. He had no sooner mentioned Dorothy's name than Lady Mottisfont showed symptoms of disquietude.

"I have not acquired any dislike of Dorothy," she said, " but I feel that there is one nearer to me now. Dorothy chose the alternative of going

to the Countess, you must remember, when I put it to her as between the Countess and myself."

"But, my dear Philippa, how can you argue thus about a child, and that child our Dorothy ?"

" Not ours,"" said his wife, pointing to the cot. " Ours is here."

" What, then, Philippa," he said, surprised, " you won't have her back, after nearly dying of grief at the loss of her?"

" I cannot argue, dear Ashley. I should prefer not to have the responsibility of Dorothy again. Iler place is filled now."

Her husband sighed, and went out of the chamber. There had been a previous arrangement that Dorothy should be brought to the house on a visit that day, but instead of taking her up to his wife, he did not inform Lady Mottisfont of the child's presence. lie entertained her himself as well as he could, and accompanied her into the park, where they had a ramble together. Presently he sat down on the root of an elm and took her upon his knee.

"Between this husband and this baby, little Dorothy, you who had two homes are left out in the cold," he said.

" Can't I go to London with my pretty mamma?" said Dorothy, perceiving from his manner that there was a liitch somewhere.

" I am afraid not, my child. She only took
you to live with her because she was lonely, you
know." 11

166 A GROUP OF NOBLB DAMES.

"Then can't I stay at Deansleigh Park with my other mamma and you?"

" I am afraid that cannot be done either," said he, sadly. " We have a baby in the house now." He closed the reply by stooping down and kissing her, there being a tear in his eye.

" Then nobody wants me!" said Dorothy, pathetically.

" Oh yes, somebody wants you," he assured her. "Where would you like to live besides?"

Dorothy's experiences being rather limited, she mentioned the only other place in the world that she was acquainted with—the cottage of the villager who had taken care of her before Lady Mottisfont had removed her to the Manor-house.

" Yes ; that's where you'll be best off and most independent," he answered. "And I'll come to see you, my dear girl, and bring you pretty things; and perhaps you'll be just as happy there."

Nevertheless, when the change came, and Dorothy was handed over to the kind cottage-woman, the poor child missed the luxurious roominess of Fernell Hall and Deansleigh; and for a long time her little feet, which had been accustomed to carpets and oak floors, suffered from the cold of the stone flags on which it was now her lot to live and to play; while chilblains came upon her fingers with washing at the pump. But thicker shoes with nails in them somewhat remedied the cold feet, and her complaints and tears on this

and other scores diminished to silence as she became inured anew to the hardships of the farm-cottage, and she grew up robust if not handsome. She was never altogether lost sight of by Sir Ashley, though she was deprived of the systematic education which had been devised and begun for her by Lady Mottisfont, as well as by her other mamma, the enthusiastic Countess. The latter soon had other Dorothys to think of, who occupied her time and affection as fully as Lady Mot-tisfont's were occupied by her precious boy. In the course of time the donbly-desired and doubly-rejected Dorothy married, I believe, a respectable road-contractor—the same, if I mistake not, who repaired and improved the old highway running from Wintoncester south-westerly through the NcAV Forest—and in the heart of this worthy man of business the poor girl found the nest which had been denied her by her own flesh and blood of higher degree.

Several of the listeners wished to hear another story from the sentimental member after this, but he said that he could recall nothing else at the moment, and that it seemed to him as if his friend on the other side of the fireplace had something to say from the look of his face.

The member alluded to was a respectable church-warden, with a sly chink to one eyelid— possibly the result of an accident—and a regular

attendant at the Club meetings. He replied that his looks had been mainly caused by his interest in the two ladies of the last story, apparently women of strong motherly instincts, even though they were not genuinely stanch in their tenderness. The tale had brought to his mind an instance of a firmer affection of that sort on the paternal side, in a nature otherwise culpable. As for telling the story, his manner was much against him, he feared ; but he would do his best, if they wished.

Here the president interposed with a suggestion that as it was getting late in the afternoon it would be as well to adjourn to their respective inns and lodgings for dinner, after which those who cared to do so could return and resume these curious domestic traditions for the remainder of the evening, which might otherwise prove irksome enough. The curator had told him that the room was at their service. The church-warden, who was beginning to feel hungry himself, readily acquiesced, and the Club separated for an hour and a half. Then the faithful ones began to drop in again—among whom were not the president; neither came the rural dean, nor the two curates, though the colonel, and the man of family, cigars in mouth, were good enough to return, having found their hotel dreary. The museum had no regular means of illumination, and a solitary candle, less powerful than the rays of the fire, was placed on the table ; also bottles and glasses, pro-

vided by some thoughtful member. The chink-eyed church-warden, now thorouglily primed, proceeded to relate, in his own terms, what was in substance as follows, while many of his listeners smoked.

part flir,
AFTER DINNER.
\
DAME THE FIFTH.
Ube Xa^B Hcenwa^?.
BY THE CHUKCH-WARDEN.

In the reign of His Most Excellent Majesty King George the Third, Defender of the Faith and of the American Colonies, there lived in "a faire maner-place " (so Leland called it in his day, as I have been told), in one o' the greenest bits of woodland between Bristol and the city of Exon-bury, a young lady who resembled some aforesaid ones in having many talents and exceeding great beauty. With these gifts she combined a somewhat imperious temper and arbitrary mind, though her experience of the world was not actually so large as her conclusive manner would have led the stranger to suppose. Being an orphan, she resided with her uncle, who, though he was fairly considerate as to her welfare, left her pretty much to herself.

Now, it chanced that when this lovely young lady was about nineteen, she (being a fearless horsewoman) was riding, with only a young lad as an attendant, in one o' the woods near her uncle's house, and, in trotting along, her horse stumbled over the root of a felled tree. She slipped to the gi'ound, not seriously hurt, and was assisted home by a gentleman who came in view at the moment of her mishap. It turned out that this gentleman, a total stranger to her, was on a visit at the house of a neighboring land-owner. He was of Dutch extraction, and occasionally came to England on business or pleasure from his plantations in Glii-ana, on the north coast of South America, where he usually resided.

On this account he was naturally but little known in Wessex, and was but a slight acquaintance of the gentleman at whose mansion he was a guest. However, the friendship between him and the Heymeres—as the uncle and niece were named — warmed and warmed by degrees, there being but few folk o' note in the vicinit\'7d^ at that time, which made a new-comer, if he were at all sociable and of good credit, always sure of a welcome. A tender feeling (as it is called by the romantic) sprang up between the two young people, which ripened into intimacy. Anderling, the foreign gentleman, was of an amorous temperament, and, though he endeavored to conceal his feeling, it could be seen that Miss Maria Heymere had impressed him rather more deeply than would be represented by a scratch upon a stone. He seemed absolutely unable to free himself from her fascination; and his inability to do so, much as he^Kd—evidently thinking he had not the ghost 0^1 chance with her—gave her the pleasure of power ; though she more than sympathized when she overheard him heaving his deep-drawn sighs—privately to himself, as he supposed.

After prolonging his visit by every conceivable excuse in his power, he summoned courage, and offered her his hand and his heart. Being in no way disinclined to him, though not so fervid as he, and her uncle making no objection to the match, she consented to share his fate, for better or otherwise, in the distant colony where, as he assured her, his rice and coffee and maize and timber produced him ample means — a statement which was borne out by his friend, her uncle's neighbor. In short, a day for their marriage was fixed, earlier in the engagement than is usual or desirable between comparative strangers, by reason of the necessity he was under of returning to look after his properties.

The wedding took place, and Maria left her uncle's mansion with her husband, going in the first place to London, and about a fortnight after sailing with him across the great ocean for their distant home—which, however, he assured her should not be her home for long, it being his intention to dispose of his interests in this part of the world as soon as the war was over and he could do so advantageously, when they could come to Europe, and reside in some favorite capital.

As they advanced on the voyage she observed that he grew more and more constrained; and by the time they had crossed the line he was quite depressed, just as he had been before proposing to lier. A day or two before landing at Paramaribo he embraced her in a very tearful and passionate manner, and said be wished to make a confession. It had been his misfortune, he said, to marry at Quebec in early life a woman whose reputation proved to be in every way bad and scandalous. The discovery had nearly killed him; but he had ultimately separated from her, and had never seen her since. He had hoped and prayed she might be dead, but recently in London, when they were starting on this journey, he had discovered that she was still alive. At first he had decided to keep this dark intelligence from her beloved ears, but he had felt that he could not do it. All he hoped was that such a condition of things would make no difference in her feelings for him, as it need make no difference in the coui'se of their lives.

Thereupon the spirit of this proud and masterful lady showed itself in violent turmoil, like the raginof of a nor'-west thunder-storm—as well it might, God knows. But she was of too stout a nature to be broken down by his revelation, as many ladies of my acquaintance would have been —so far from home and right under the line in the blaze o' the sun. Of the two, indeed, he was the more wretched and shattered in spirit, for he loved her deeply, and (there being a foreign twist

in his make) had been tempted to this crime by her exceeding beauty, against which he had struggled day and night, till he had no further resistance left in him. It was she who came first to a decision as to what should be done—whether a wise one I do not attempt to judge.

" I put it to you," says she, when many useless self-reproaches and protestations on his part had been uttered—" I put it to you whether, if any manliness is left in you, you ought not to do exactly what I consider the best thing for me in this strait to which you have reduced me ?"

He promised to do anything in the whole world. She then requested him to allow her to return and announce hira as having died of malignant ague immediately on their arrival at Paramaribo; that she should consequently appear in weeds as his widow in her native place; and that he would never molest her, or come again to that part of the world during the whole course of his life—a good reason for which would be that the legal consequences might be serious.

He readily acquiesced in this, as he would have acquiesced in anything for the restitution of one he adored so deeply—even to the yielding of life itself. To put her in an immediate state of inde-pcndonee he gave her, in bonds and jewels, a considerable sum (for his worldly means had been in no way exaggerated), and by the next ship she sailed again for England, having travelled no farther than to Paramaribo, At parting he declared

it to be his intention to turn all his landed possessions into personal property, and to be a wanderer on the face of the earth in remorse for his conduct towards her.

Maria duly arrived in England, and immediately on landing apprised her uncle of her return, duly appearing at his house in the garb of a widow. She was commiserated by all the neighbors as soon as her story was told; but only to her uncle did she reveal the real state of affairs and her reason for concealing it. For, though she had been innocent of wrong, Maria's pride was of that grain which could not brook the least appearance of having been fooled or deluded or nonplussed in her worldly aims.

For some time she led a quiet life with her relative, and in due course a son was born to her. She was much respected for her dignity and reserve, and the portable wealth which her temporary husband had made over to her enabled her to live in comfort in a wing of the mansion, without assistance from her uncle at all. But, knowing that she was not what she seemed to be, her life was an uneasy one, and she often said to herself: "Suppose his continued existence should become known here, and people should discern the pride of my motive in hiding my humiliation ? It would be worse than if I had been frank at first, which I should have been but for the credit of this child."

Such grave reflections as these occupied her with increasing force; and during their continuance she encountered a worthy man of noble birth and title—Lord Icenway his name—whose seat was beyond Wintoncester, quite at t'other end of Wessex. He being anxious to pay his addresses to her, Maria willingly accepted them, though he was a plain man, older than herself, for she discerned in a remarriage a method of fortifying her position against mortifying discoveries. In a few months their union took place, and Maria lifted her head as Lady Icenway, and left with her husband and child for his home as aforesaid, where she was quite unknown.

A justification, or a condemnation, of her step (according as you view it) was seen when, not long after, she received a note from her former husband Andcrling. It was a hasty and tender epistle, and perhaps it was fortunate that it arrived during the temporary absence of Lord Icenway. His worthless wife, said Andcrling, had just died in Quebec; he had gone there to ascertain particulai's, and had seen the unfortunate woman buried. He now was hastening to England to repair the wrong he had done liis Maria. He asked her to meet him at Southampton, his port of arrival; which she need be in no fear of doing, as he had changed his name, and was almost absolutely unknown in Europe. He would remarry her immediately, and live with her in any part of the Continent, as they had originally intended, where, for the great love he still bore her, he would devote himself to her service for the rest of his days.

Lady Icenway, self-possessed as it was her nature to be, was yet much disturbed at this news, and set off to meet him, unattended, as soon as she heard that the ship was in sight. As soon as they stood face to face she found that she still possessed all her old influence over him, though his power to fascinate her had quite departed. In his sorrow for his offence against her, he had become a man of strict religious habits, self-denying as a lenten saint, though formerly he had been a free and joyous liver. Having first got him to swear to make her any amends she should choose (which he was imagining must be by a true marriage), she informed him that she had already wedded another husband, an excellent man of ancient family and possessions, who had given her a title, in which she much rejoiced.

At this the countenance of the poor foreign gentleman became cold as clay, and his heart withered within him; for as it had been her beauty and bearing which had led him to sin to obtain her, so, now that her beauty was in fuller bloom, and her manner more haughty by her success, did he feel her fascination to be almost more than he could bear. Nevertheless, having sworn his word, he undertook to obey her commands, which were simply a renewal of her old request — that he would depart for some foreign country, and never reveal his existence to her friends, or husband, or any person in England; never trouble her more, seeing how great a harm it would do her in the high position which she at present occupied.

He bowed his head, "And the child — our child ?" he said.

"He is well," says she—"quite well."

With this the unhappy gentleman departed, much sadder in his heart than on his voyage to England; for it had never occurred to him that a woman who rated her honor so highly as Maria had done, and who was the mother of a child of his, would have adopted such means as this for the restoration of that honor, and at so surprisingly early a date. He had fully calculated on making her his wife in law and truth, and of living in cheerful unity with her and his offspring, for whom he felt a deep and growing tenderness, though he had never once seen the child.

The lady returned to her mansion beyond Win-toncester, and told nothing of the interview to her noble husband, who had fortunately gone that day to do a little cocking and ratting out by Weydon Priors and knew nothing of her movements. She had dismissed her poor Anderling peremptorily enough; yet she would often after this look in the face of the child of her so-called widowhood, to discover what and how many traits of his father were to be seen in his lineaments. For this she had ample opportunity during the following autumn and winter months, her husband being a matter-of-fact nobleman, who spent the greater part of his time in field sports and agriculture.

One winter day, when he had started for a meet of the hounds a long way from the house—it being his custom to hunt three or four times a week at this season of the year—she had walked into the sunshine upon the terrace before the windows, where there fell at her feet some little white object that had come over a boundary wall hard by. It proved to be a tiny note wrapped round a stone. Lady Icenway opened it and read it, and immediately (no doubt with a stern fixture of her queenly countenance) walked hastily along the terrace, and through the door into the shrubbery, whence the note had come. The man who had first married her stood under the bushes before her. It was plain from his appearance that something had gone wrong with him.

" You notice a change in me, my best-beloved," he said. " Yes, Maria, I have lost all the wealth I once possessed, mainly by reckless gambling in the Continental hells to which you banished me. But one thing in the world remains to me—the child—and it is for bim that I have intruded here. Don't fear me, darling. I shall not inconvenience you long; I love you too well. But I think of the boy day and night—I cannot help it—I cannot keep my feeling for him down; and I long to see him and speak a word to him once in my lifetime!"

"But your oath?" says she. "You promised never to reveal by word or sign—"

" I will reveal nothing. Only let me see the child. I know what I have sworn to you, cruel mistress, and I respect my oath. Otherwise I might have seen him by some subterfuge. But I preferred the frank course of asking your permission."

She demurred, with the haughty severity which had grown part of her character, and which her elevation to the rank of a peeress had rather intensified than diminished. She said that she would consider, and would give him an answer the day after the next, at the same hour and place, when her husband would again be absent with his pack of hounds.

The gentleman waited patiently. Lady Icen-way, who had now no conscious love left for him, well considered the matter, and felt that it would be advisable not to push to extremes a man of so passionate a heart. On the day and hour she met him, as she had promised to do.

" You shall see him," she said ; " of course on the strict condition that you do not reveal yourself, and hence, though you see him, he must not see you, or your manner might betray you and me. I will lull him into a nap in the afternoon, and then I will come to you here, and fetch you in-doors by a private way."

The unfortunate fatlier, whose misdemeanor had recoiled upon his own head in a way he could not have foreseen, promised to adhere to her instructions, and waited in the shrubberies till the moment when she should call him. This she duly did about three o'clock that day, leading him in by a garden door, and up-stairs to the nursery where the child lay. He was in his little cot, breathing calmly, his arm thrown over his head, and his silken curls crushed into the pillow. His father, now almost to be pitied, bent over him, and a tear from his eye wetted the coverlet.

She held up a warning finger as he lowered his mouth to the lips of the boy.

" But oh, why not ?" implored he.

" Very well, then," said she, relenting. " But as gently as possible."

He kissed the child without waking him, turned, gave him a last look, and followed her out of the chamber, when she conducted him off the premises by the way he had come.

But this remedy for his sadness of heart at being a stranger to his own son had the effect of intensifying the malady; for while originally— not knowing or ever having seen the boy — he had loved him vaguely and imaginative!\'7d^ only, he now became attached to him in flesh and bone, as any parent might; and the feeling that he could at best only see his child at the rarest and most cursory moments, if at all, drove him into a state of distraction which threatened to overthrow his promise to the boy's mother to keep out of his sight. But such was his chivalrous respect for Lady Icenway, and his regret at having ever deceived her, that he schooled his poor heart

into submission. Owing to his loneliness, all the fervor of which he was cajiable—and that was much—flowed now in the channel of parental and marital love—for a child who did not know him, and a woman who had ceased to love him.

At length this singular punishment became such a torture to the poor foreigner that he resolved to lessen it at all hazards compatible wnth punctilious care for the name of the lady, his former wife, to whom his attachment seemed to increase in proportion to her punitive treatment of him. At one time of his life he had taken great interest in tulip-culture, as well as gardening in general; and since the ruin of his fortunes, and his arrival in England, he had made of his knowledge a precarious income in the hot-houses of nurserymen and others. With the now idea in his head he applied himself zealously to the business, till he acquired in a few months great skill in horticulture. Waiting till the noble lord, his lady's husband, had room for an under-gardener of a general sort, he offered himself for the place, and was engaged immediately by reason of his civility and intelligence, before Lady Iccnway knew anything of the matter. Much, therefore, did he surjjrise her when she found him in the conservatories of her mansion a week or two after his arrival. Tlie punishment of instant dismissal, with which at first she haughtily threatened liiin, my lady thought fit, on reflection, not to enforce. While he served her thus she knew he would not

harm her by a word, while, if he were expelled, chagrin might induce him to reveal in a moment of exasperation what kind treatment would assist him to conceal.

So he was allowed to remain on the premises, and had for his residence a little cottage by the garden wall vvhich had been the domicile of some of his predecessors in the same occupation. Here he lived absolutely alone, and spent much of his leisure in reading, but the greater part in watching the windows and lawns of his lady's house for glimpses of the form of the child. It was for that child's sake that he abandoned the tenets of the Roman Catholic Church in which he had been reared, and became the most regular attendant at the services in the parish place of worship hard by, where, sitting behind the pew of my lady, ray lord, and his step-son, the gardener could pensively study the traits and movements of the youngster at only a few feet distance, without suspicion or hinderance. ^

He filled his post for more than two years with a pleasure to himself which, though mournful, was soothing, his lady never forgiving him or allowing him to be anything more than " the gardener " to her child, though once or twice the boy said: " That gardener's eyes are so sad ! Why does he look so sadly at me ?" He sunned himself in her scornf ulness as if it were love, and his ears drank in her curt monosyllables as though they were rhapsodies of endearment. Strangely

enough, the coldness with which she treated her foreigner began to be the conduct of Lord Icen-way towards herself. It was a matter of great anxiety to him that there should be a lineal successor to the title, yet no sign of that successor appeared. One day he complained to her quite roughly of his fate. "All will go to that dolt of a cousin!" he cried. "I'd sooner see my name and place at the bottom of the sea!"

The lady soothed him and fell into thought, and did not recriminate. But one day, soon after, she went down to the cottage of the gardener to inquire how he was getting on, for he had been ailing of late, though, as was supposed, not seriously. Though she often visited the poor, she had never entered her under-gardener's home before, and was much surprised—even grieved and dismayed—to find that he was too ill to rise from his bed. She went back to her mansion, and returned with some delicate soup, that she might have a reason fqn seeing him.

His condition was so feeble and alarming, and his face so thin, that it quite shocked her softening heart, and gazing upon him, she said: "You must get well — you must! I have been hard with you—I know it. I will not be so again."

The sick and dying man—for he was dying indeed—took her hand and pressed it to his lips. "Too late, my darling, too late!" he murmured.

"But you must not die! Oh, you must not!" she said. And on an impulse she bent dowo and

whispered some words to him, blushing as she had blushed in her maiden days.

He replied by a faint, wan smile. "Time was! . . . but that's past," he said. "I must die!"

And die he did, a few days later, as the sun was going down behind the garden wall. Her harshness seemed to come trebly home to her then, and she remorsefully exclaimed against herself in secret and alone. Her one desire now was to erect some tribute to his memory, without its being recognized as her handiwork. In the completion of this scheme there arrived a few months later a handsome stained-glass window for the church; and when it was unpacked and in course of erection Lord Icenway strolled into the building with his wife.

"' Erected to his tneniory by his grieving wid-010,'" he said, reading the legend on the glass. "I didn't know that he had a wife; I've never seen her."

"Oh yes, you must have, Icenway, only you forget," replied his lady, blandly. "But she didn't live with him, and was seldom seen visiting him, because there were differences between them; which, as is usually the case, makes her all^ the more sorry now."

"And go ruining herself by this expensive ruby-and-azure glass design."

"She is not poor, they say."

As Lord Icenway grew older he became crustier and crustier, and whenever he set eyes on his wife's boy by her other husband he would burst out morosely, saying:

"'Tis a very odd thing, my lady, that you could oblige your first husband, and couldn't oblige me."

"Ah, if I bad only thought of it sooner!" she murmured.

"What?" said he.

"Nothing, dearest," replied Lady Icenway,

The colonel was the first to comment upon the churcli-warden's t:ile, by saying that the fate of the poor fellow was rather a hard one.

The gentleman-tradesman could not see that his fate was at all too hard for him. He was legally nothing to her, and he had served her shamefully. If he had been really her husband it would have stood differently.

The bookworm remarked that Lord IcenAvay seemed to have been a ver\'7d" unsuspicious man, with which view a fat member with a crimson face agreed. It was true his wife was a very close-mouthed personage, which made a difference. If she had spoken out recklessly her lord might have been suspicious enough, as in the case of that lady who lived at Stapleford Park in their great-grandfathers' time. Though there, to be sure, considerations arose which made her husband view matters with much philosophy.

A few of tlie members doubted the possibility of this.

The crimson man, who was a retired maltster of comfortable means, vetitrii, and short in stature, cleared his throat, blew off his superfluous breath, and proceeded to give the instance before alluded to of such possibility, first apologizing for his heroine's lack of a title, it never having been his good-fortune to know many of the nobility. To his style of narrative the following is only an approximation.

DAME THE SIXTH.

Squire jpetrlcft's %a^^,

BY THE CRIMSON MALTSTER.

Folk who are at all acquainted with the traditions of Stapleford Park will not need to be told that in the middle of the last centurj'- it was owned by that trump of mortgagees, Timothy Petrick, whose skill in gaining possession of fair estates by granting sums of money on their title-deeds has seldom if ever been equalled in our part of England. Timothy was a lawyer by profession, and agent to several noblemen, by which means his special line of business became opened to him by a sort of revelation. It is said that a relative of his, a very deep thinker, who afterwards had the misfortune to be transported for life for mistaken notions on the signing of a will, taught him considerable legal lore, which he creditably resolved never to throw away for the benefit of other people, but to reserve it entirely for his own.

However, I have nothing in particular to say

about his early and active days, but rather of the time when, an old man, he had become the owner of vast estates by the means I have signified— among them the great manor of Stapleford, on which he lived, in the splendid old mansion now pulled down ; likewise estates at Marlott, estates near Sherton Abbas, nearly all the borough of Millpool, and many properties near Ivell. Indeed, I can't call to mind half his landed possessions, and I don't know that it matters much at this time of day, seeing that he's been dead and gone many years. It is said that when he bought an estate he would not decide to pay the price till he had walked over every single acre with his own two feet, and prodded the soil at every point with his own spud, to test its quality, which, if we regard the extent of his properties, must have been a stiff business for him.

At the time I am speaking of he was a man over eighty, and his son was dead; but he had two grandsons, the eldest of whom, his namesake, was married, and was shortly expecting issue. Just then the grandfather was taken ill, for death, as it seemed, considering his age. By his will the old man had created an entail (as I believe the lawyers call it), devising the whole of the estates to his elder grandson and his issue male, failing which, to his younger grandson and his issue male, failing which, to remoter relatives, who need not be mentioned now.

While old Timothy Petrick was lying ill, his

elder grandson's wife, Annetta, gave birth to her expected child, who, as fortune would have it, was a son, Timothy, her husband, tbough sprung of a scheming family, was no great schemer himself; he was the single one of the Petricks then living whose heart had ever been greatly moved by sentiments which did not run in the groove of ambition; and on this account he had not married well, as the saying is, his wife having been the daughter of a family of no better beginnings than his own; that is to say, her father was a country townsman of the professional class. But she was a very pretty woman, by all accounts, and her husband had seen, courted, and married her in a high tide of infatuation, after a very short acquaintance, and with very little knowledge of her heart's history. lie had never found reason to regret his choice as yet, and his anxiety for her recovery was great.

She was supposed to be out of danger, and herself and the child progressing well, when there was a change for the worse, and she sank so rapidly that she was soon given over. When she felt that she was about to leave him, Annetta sent for her husband, and, on his speedy entry and assurance that they were alone, she made him solemnly vow to give the child every care in any circumstances that might arise, if it should please Heaven to take her. This, of course, he readily promised. Then, after some hesitation, she told him that she could not die with a falsehood upon 13

her soul, and dire deceit in her life; she must make a terrible confession to him before her lips were sealed forever. She thereupon related an incident concerning the baby's parentage which was not as he supposed.

Timothy Petrick, though a quick-feeling man, was not of a sort to show nerves outwardly; and he bore himself as heroically as he possibly could do in this trying moment of his life. That same night his wife died; and while she lay dead, and before her funeral, he hastened to the bedside of his sick grandfather, and revealed to him all that had happened—the baby's birth, his wife's confession, and her death, beseeching the aged man, as he loved him, to bestir himself now, at the eleventh hour, and alter his will so as to dish the intruder. Old Timothy, seeing matters in the same light as his gi'andson, required no urging against allowing anything to stand in the way of legitimate inheritance; he executed another will, limiting the entail to Timothy, his grandson, for life, and his male heirs thereafter to be born; after them to his other grandson, Edward, and Edward's heirs. Thus the newly-born infant, who had been the centre of so many hopes, was cut off and scorned as none of the elect.

The old mortgagee lived but a short time after this, the excitement of the discovery having told upon him considerably, and he was gathered to his fathers like the most charitable man in his neighborhood. Both wife and grandparent being buried, Timothy settled down to his usual life as well as he was able, mentally satisfied that he had, by promj^t action, defeated the consequences of such dire domestic treachery as had been shown towards him, and resolving to marry a second time as soon as he could satisfy himself in the choice of a wife.

But men do not always know themselves. The imbittered state of Timothy Petrick's mind bred in him by degrees such a hatred and mistrust of womankind that, though several specimens of high attractiveness- came under his eyes, he could not bring himself to the point of projiosing marriage. He dreaded to take up the position of husband a second time, discerning a trap in every petticoat, and a Slough of Despond in possible heirs. " What has happened once, when all seemed so fair, may happen again," he said to himself. " I'll risk my name no more." So he abstained from marriage, and overcame his wish for a lineal descendant to follow him in the ownership of Sta-pleford.

Timothy had scarcely noticed the unfortunate child that his wife had borne, after arranging for a meagre fulfilment of his promise to her to take care of the boy, by having him brought up in his house. Occasionally, remembering this promise, he went and glanced at the child, saw that he was doing well, gave a few special directions, and again went his solitary way.

Thus he and the child lived on in the Stapleford mansion-house till two or three years had passed by. One day he was walking in the garden, and by some accident left his snuffbox on a bench. When he came back to find it he saw the little boy standing there ; he had escaped his nurse, and was making a plaything of the box, in spite of the convulsive sneezings which the game brought in its train. Then the man with the incrusted heart became interested in the little fellow's persistence in his play under such discomforts ; he looked in the child's face, saw there his wife's countenance, though he did not see his own, and fell into thought on the piteousness of childhood—particularly of despised and rejected childhood, like this before him.

From that hour, try as he would to counteract the feeling, the human necessity to love something or other got the better of what he had called his wisdom, and shaped itself in a tender anxiety for the youngster Rupert. This name had been given him by his dying mother when, at her request, the child was baptized in her chamber, lest he should not survive for public baptism ; and her husband had never thought of it as a name of any significance till, about this time, he learned by accident that it was the name of the young Marquis of Christminster, son of the Duke of Southwester-land, for whom Annetta had cherished warm feelings before her marriage. Recollecting some wandering phrases in his wife's last words, which he had not understood at the time, he perceived as last that this was the person to whom she had alluded when affording him a clew to little Rupert's history.

He would sit in silence for hours with the child, being no great speaker at the best of times; but the boy, on his part, was too ready with his tongue for any break in discourse to arise because Timothy Petrick had nothing to say. After idling away his mornings in this manner, Petrick would go to his own room and swear in long, loud whispers, and walk up and down, calling himself the most ridiculous dolt that ever lived, and declaring that he would never go near the little fellow again; to which resolve he would adhere for the space, perhaps, of a day. Such cases are happily not new to human nature, but there never was a case in which a man more completely befooled his former self than in this.

As the child grew up, Timothy's attachment to him grew deeper, till Rupert became almost the sole object for which he lived. There had been enough of the family ambition latent in him for Timothy Petrick to feel a little envy when, some time before this date, his brother Edward had been accepted by the Honorable Harriet Mount-clere, daughter of the second viscount of that name and title ; but having discovered, as I have before stated, the paternity of his boy Rupert to lurk in even a higher stratum of society, those envious feelings speedily dispersed. Indeed, the more he reflected thereon, after his brother's aristocratic marriage, the more content did he become. His late wife took softer outline in his memory, as he thought of the lofty taste she had displayed, though only a plain burgher's daughter, and the justification for his weakness in loving the child— the justification that he had longed for—was afforded now in the knowledge that the boy was by nature, if not by name, a representative of one of the noblest houses in England.

"She was a woman of grand instincts, after all," he said to himself, proudly. "To fix her choice upon the immediate successor in that ducal line—it was finely conceived! Had he been of low blood like myself or my relations she would scarce have deserved the harsh measure that I have dealt out to her and her offspring. How much less, then, when such grovelling tastes were farthest from her soul! The man Annetta loved was noble, and my boy is noble in spite of me."

The after-clap was inevitable, and it soon came. "So far," he reasoned, "from cutting off this child from inheritance of my estates, as I have done, I should have rejoiced in the possession of him ! He is of pure stock on one side at least, while in the ordinary run of affairs he would have been a commoner to the bone."

Being a man, whatever his faults, of good old beliefs in the divinity of kings and those about 'em, the more he overhauled the case in this light the more strongly did his poor wife's conduct in improving the blood and breed of the Petrick

family win his heart. He considered what ugly, idle, hard-drinking scamps many of his own relations had been; the miserable scriveners, usurers, and pawnbrokers that he had numbered among his forefathers, and the probability that some of their bad qualities would have come out in a merely corporeal child, to give him sorrow in his old age, turn his black hairs gray, his gray hairs white, cut down every stick of timber, and Heaven knows what all, had he not, like a skilful gardener, minded his grafting and changed the sort; till at length this right-minded man fell down on his knees every night and morning and thanked God that he was not as other meanly-descended fathers in such matters.

It was in the peculiar disposition of the Petrick family that the satisfaction which ultimately settled in Timothy's breast found nourishment. The Petricks had adored the nobility, and plucked them at the same time. That excellent man Izaak Walton's feelings about fish were much akin to those of old Timothy Petrick, and of his descendants in a lesser degree, concerning the landed aristocracy. To torture and to love simultaneously is a proceeding strange to reason, but possible to practice, as these instances show.

Hence, when Timothy's brother Edward said slightingly one day that Timothy's son was well enough, but that he had nothing but shops and oHices in his backward perspective, while his own children, should he have any, would be far differ-

ent, in possessing such a mother as the Honorable Harriet, Timothy felt a bonnd of triumph within him at the power he possessed of contradicting that statement if he chose.

So much was he interested in his boy in this new aspect that he now began to read up chronicles of the illustrious house ennobled as the Dukes of Soutliwesterland, from their very beginning in the glories of the Restoration of the blessed Charles till the year of his own time. He mentally noted their gifts from royalty, grants of lands, purchases, intermarriages, plantings, and buildings ; more particularly their political and military achievements, which had been great, and their performances in arts and letters, which had been by no means contemptible. He studied prints of the poi'traits of that family, and then, like a chemist watching a crystallization, began to examine young Rupert's face for the unfolding of those historic curves and shades that the painters Vandyke and Lely had perpetuated on canvas.

When the boy reached the most fascinating age of childhood, and his shouts of laughter ran through Stapleford House from end to end, the remorse that oppressed Timothy Petrick knew no bounds. Of all people in the world this Rupert was the one on whom he could have wished the estates to devolve ; yet Rupert, by Timothy's own desperate strategy at the time of his birth, had been ousted from all inheritance of them ; and, since he did not mean to remarry, the manors

would pass to his brother and his brother's children, who would be nothing to him, Avhose boasted pedigree on one side would be nothing to his Rupert's.

Had he only left the first will of his grandfather alone!

His mind ran on the wills continually, both of which were in existence, and the first, the cancelled one, in his own possession. Night after night, Avhen the servants were all abed, and the click of safety-locks sounded as loud as a crash, he looked at that first will, and wished it had been the second and not the first.

The crisis came at last. One night, after having enjoyed the boy's company for hours, he could no longer bear that his beloved Rupert should be dispossessed, and he committed the felonious deed of altering the date of the earlier will to a fortnight later, which made its execution appear subsequent to the date of the second will already proved. He then boldly propounded the first will as the second.

His brother Edward submitted to what appeared to be not only incontestible fact, but a far more likely disposition of old Timothy's property; for, like many others, he had been much surprised at the limitations defined in the other will, having no clew to their cause. He joined his brother Timothy in setting aside the hitherto accepted document, and matters went on in their usual course, there being no dispositions in the substi-

tuted will differing from those in the other, except such as related to a future which had not yet arrived.

The years moved on. Rupert had not yet revealed the anxiously-expected historic lineaments which should foreshadow the political abilities of the ducal family aforesaid, when it happened on a certain day that Timothy Petrick made the acquaintance of a well-known physician of Bud-mouth, who had been the medical adviser and friend of the late Mrs. Petrick's family for many years, though after Annetta's marriage, and consequent removal to Staplefoi'd, he had seen no more of her, the neighboring practitioner who attended the Petricks having then become her doctor as a matter of course. Timothy was impressed by the insight and knowledge disclosed in the conversation of the Budmouth physician, and the acquaintance ripening to intimacy, the physician alluded to a form of hallucination to which Annetta's mother and grandmother had been subject —that of believing in certain dreams as realities. He delicately inquired if Timothy had ever noticed anything of the sort in his wife during her lifetime; he, the physician, had fancied that he discerned germs of the same peculiarity in Annet-ta when he attended her in her girlhood. One explanation begat another, till the dumfounded Timothy Petrick was persuaded in his own mind that Annetta's confession to him had been based on a delusion.

"You look down in the mouth!" said the doctor, pausing.

"A bit unmanned. 'Tis unexpected-like," sighed Timothy.

But he could hardly believe it possible; and, thinking it best to be frank with the doctor, told him the whole story which, till now, he had never related to living man, save his dying grandfather. To his surprise, the physician informed him that such a form of delusion was precisely what he would have expected from Annetta's antecedents at such a physical crisis in her life.

Petrick prosecuted his inquiries elsewhere; and the upshot of his labors was, briefly, that a comparison of dates and places showed irrefutably that his poor wife's assertion could not possibly have foundation in fact. The young Marquis of her tender passion—a highly moral and bright-minded nobleman—had gone abroad the year before Annetta's marriage, and had not returned until after her death. The young girl's love for him had been a delicate ideal dream—no more.

Timothy went home, and the boy ran out to meet him; whereupon a strangely dismal feeling of discontent took possession of his soul. After all, then, there was nothing but plebeian blood in the veins of the heir to his name and estates; he was not to be succeeded by a noble-natured line. To be sure, Rupert was his son; but that glor'7d' and halo he believed him to have inherited from the ages, outshining that of his brother's children, had departed from Rupert's brow forever; he could no longer read history in the boy's face and centuries of domination in his eyes.

His manner towards his son grew colder and colder from that day forward; and it was with bitterness of heart that he discerned the characteristic features of the Petricks unfolding themselves by degrees. Instead of the elegant knife-edged nose, so typical of the Dukes of South-westerland, there began to appear on his face the broad nostril and hollow bridge of his grandfather Timothy. No illustrious line of politicians was promised a continuator in that graying blue eye, for it was acquiring the expression of the orb of a particularly objectionable cousin of his own; and, instead of the mouth-curves which had thrilled Parliamentary audiences in speeches now bound in calf in every well-ordered library, there was the bull-lip of that very uncle of his who had had the misfortune with the signature of a gentleman's will, and had been transported for life in consequence.

To think how he himself, too, had sinned in this same matter of a will for this mere fleshly reproduction of a wretched old uncle whose very name he wished to forget! The boy's Christian name, even, was an imposture and an irony, for it implied hereditary force and brilliancy to which he plainly would never attain. The consolation of real sonship was always left him certainly; but he could not help groaning to himself, " Why cannot a son be one's own and somebody else's likewise ?"

The Marquis was shortly afterwards in the neighborhood of Stapleford, and Timothy Petrick met him, and eyed his noble countenance admiringly. The next day, when Petrick was in his study, somebody knocked at the door.

" Who's there ?"

" Rupert."

" ril Rupert thee, you young impostor! Say, only a poor commonplace Petrick !" his father grunted. " Why didn't you have a voice like the Marquis I saw yesterday?" he continued, as the lad came in. " Why haven't you his looks, and a way of commanding as if you'd done it for centuries—hey ?"

" Why ? How can you expect it, father, when I'm not related to him?"

'* Ugh ! Then you ought to be !" growled his father.

As the narrator paused, the surgeon, the colonel, the historian, the Spark, and others exclaimed that such subtle and instructive psychological studies as this (now that psychology was so much in demand) were precisely the tales they desired, as members of a scientific club, and begged the master-maltster to tell another curious mental delusion.

Tlie maltster shook his head, and feared he was not genteel enough to tell another story with a sufficiently moral tone to it to suit the club; he would prefer to leave the next to a better man.

The colonel had fallen into reflection. True it was, he observed, that the more dreamy and impulsive nature of woman engendered within her erratic fancies, which often started her on strange tracks, only to abandon them in sharp revulsion at the dictates of her common-sense—sometimes with ludicrous effect. Events which had caused a lady's action to set in a particular direction might continue to enforce the same line of conduct, while she, like a mangle, would start on a sudden in a contrary course, and end where she began.

The vice-president laughed, and applauded the colonel, adding that there surely lurked a story somewhere behind that sentiment, if he were not much mistaken.

The colonel fixed his face to a good narrative pose, and went on without further preamble.

DAME THE SEVENTH.

anna, XaD^ Bajby*

BY THE COLONEL.

It was in the time of the great Civil War—if I should not rather, as a loyal subject, call it, with Clarendon, the Great Rebellion. It was, I say, at that unhappy period of our history, that towards the autumn of a particular year, the Parliament forces sat down before Sherton Castle with over seven thousand foot and four pieces of cannon. The Castle, as we all know, was in that century owned and occupied by one of the Earls of Severn, and garrisoned for his assistance by a certain noble Marquis who commanded the King's troops in these parts. The said Earl, as well as the young Lord Baxby, his eldest son, were away from home just now, raising forces for the King elsewhere. But there were present in the Castle, Avhen the besiegers arrived before it, the son's fair wife. Lady Baxby, and her servants, together with some friends and near relatives of her husband;

and the defence was so good and well-considered that they anticipated no great danger.

The Parliamentary forces were also commanded by a noble lord — for the nobility were by no means, at this stage of the war, all on the King's side—and it had been observed during his approach in the night-time, and in the morning when the reconnoitring took place, that he appeared sad and much depressed. The truth was that, by a strange freak of destiny, it had come to pass that the stronghold he was set to reduce was the home of his own sister, whom he had tenderly loved during her maidenhood, and whom he loved now, in spite of the estrangement which had resulted from hostilities with her husband's family. He believed, too, that, notwithstanding this cruel division, she still was sincerely attached to him.

His hesitation to point his ordnance at the walls was inexplicable to those who were strangers to his family history. He remained in the field on the north side of the Castle (called by his name to this day because of his encampment there) till it occurred to him to send a messenger to his sister Anna with a letter, in which he earnestly requested her, as she valued her life, to steal out of the place by the little gate to the south, and make away in that direction to the residence of some friends.

Shortly after be saw, to his great surprise, coming from the front of the Castle walls a lady on horseback, with a single attendant. She rode

straight forward into the field, and up the slope to where his army and tents were spread. It was not till she got quite near that he discerned her to be his sister Anna; and much was he alarmed that she should have run such risk as to sally out in the face of his forces without knowledge of their proceedings, when at any moment their first discharge might have burst forth, to her own destruction in such exposure. She dismounted before she was quite close to hira, and he saw that her familiar face, though pale, was not at all tearful, as it would have been in their younger days. Indeed, if the particulars as handed down are to be believed, he was in a more tearful state than she, in his anxiety about her. He called her into his tent, out of the gaze of those around ; for though many of the soldiers were honest and serious-minded men, he could not bear that she who had been his dear companion in childhood should be exposed to curious observation in this her great grief.

When they were alone in the tent he clasped her in his arms, for he had not seen her since those happier days, when, at the commencement of the war, her husband and himself had been of the same mind about the arbitrary conduct of the King, and had little dreamed that they would not go to extremes together. She was the calmest of the two, it is said, and was the first to speak connectedly.

" William, I have come to you," said she, " but not to save myself, as you suppose. Why, oh, why do you persist in supporting this disloyal cause, and grieving us so ?"

" Say not that," he replied, hastily. " If truth hides at the bottom of a well, why should you suppose justice to be in high places? I am for the right, at any price. Anna, leave the Castle ; you are my sister; come away, my dear, and save thy life!"

*' Never!" says she. " Do you plan to carry out this attack, and level the Castle indeed ?"

" Most certainly I do," says he. " What mean-eth this army around us if not so ?"

"Then you will find the bones of your sister buried in the ruins you cause!" said she. And without another word she turned and left him.

"Anna—abide with me!" he entreated. " Blood is thicker than water, and what is there in common between you and your husband now ?"

But she shook her head and would not hear him; and hastening out, mounted her horse, and returned towards the Castle as she had come. Aye, many's the time when I have been riding to hounds across that field have I thought of that scene!

When she had quite gone down the field, and over the intervening ground, and round the bastion, so that he could no longer even see the tip of her mare's white tail, he was much more deeply moved by emotions concerning her and her welfare than he had been while she was before him.

He wildly reproached himself that he had not detained her by force for her own good, so that, come what might, she would be under his protection and not under that of her husband, whose impulsive nature rendered him too open to instantaneous impressions and sudden changes of plan; he was now acting in this cause and now in that, and lacked the cool judgment necessary for the protection of a woman in these troubled times. Her brother thought of her words again and again, and sighed, and even considered if a sister were not of more value than a principle, and if he would not have acted more naturally in throwing in his lot with hers.

The delay of the besiegers in attacking the Castle was said to be entirely owing to this distraction on the part of their leader, who remained on the spot attempting some indecisive operations, and parleying with the Marquis, then in command, with far inferior forces, within the Castle. It never occurred to him that in the mean time the young Lady Baxby, his sister, was in much the same mood as himself. Her brother's familiar voice and eyes, much worn and fatigued by keeping the field, and by family distractions on account of this unhappy feud, rose upon her vision all the afternoon, and as day waned she grew more and more Parliamentarian in her principles, though the only arguments which had addressed themselves to her were those of family ties.

Her husband, General Lord Baxby, had been expected to return all the day from his excursion into the east of the county, a message having been sent to him informing him of what had happened at home; and in the evening he arrived with reinforcements in unexpected numbers. Her brother retreated before these to a hill near Ivell, four or five miles off, to afford the men and himself some repose. Lord Baxby duly placed his forces, and there was no longer any immediate danger. By this time Lady Baxby's feelings were more Parliamentarian than ever, and in her fancy the fagged countenance of her brother, beaten back by her husband, seemed to reproach her for heartless-ness. When her husband entered her apartment, ruddy and boisterous and full of hope, she received him but sadly; and upon his casually uttering some slighting words about her brother's withdrawal, which seemed to convey an imputation upon his courage, she resented them, and retorted that he, Lord Baxby himself, had been against the Court-party at first, where it would be much more to his credit if he were at present, and showing her brother's consistency of opinion, instead of supporting the lying policy of the King (as she called it) for the sake of a barren principle of loyalty, which was but an empty expression when a king was not at one with his people. The dissension grew bitter between them, reaching to little less than a hot quarrel, both being quicktempered souls. Lord Baxby was weary with his long day's march and other excitements, and soon retired to bed. His lady followed some time after. Her husband slept profoundly, but not so she; she sat brooding by the window-slit, and lifting the curtain looked forth upon the hills without.

In the silence between the footfalls of the sentinels she could hear faint sounds of her brother's camp on the distant hills, where the soldiery had hardly settled as yet into their bivouac since their evening's retreat. The first frosts of autumn had touched the grass, and shrivelled the more delicate leaves of the creepers ; and she thought of William sleeping on the chilly ground, under the strain of these hardships. Tears flooded her eyes as she returned to her husband's imputations upon his courage, as if there could be any doubt of Lord William's courage after what he had done in the jjast days.

Lord Baxby's long and reposeful breathings in his comfortable bed vexed her now, and she came to a determination on an impulse. Hastily lighting a taper, she wrote on a scrap of paper:

^^Blood is tJiiclcer than water, dear William —/ loill cotne f and with this in her hand, she Avent to the door of the room, and out upon the stairs; on second thoughts turning back for a moment, to put on her husband's hat and cloak—not the one he was daily wearing—that if seen in the twilight she might at a casual glance appear as some lad or hanger-on of one of the household women;

thus accoutred she descended a flight of circular p
Btairs, at the bottom of which was a door opening upon the terrace towards the west, in the direction of her brother's position. Her object was to slip out without the sentry seeing her, get to the stables, arouse one of the varlets, and send him ahead of her along the highway with the note to warn her brother of her approach to throw in her lot with his.

She was still in the shadow of the wall on the west terrace, waiting for the sentinel to be quite out of the way, when her ears were greeted by a voice, saying, from the adjoining shade :

" Here I be!"

The tones were the tones of a woman. Lady Baxby made no reply, and stood close to the wall.

" My Lord Baxby," the voice continued; and she could recognize in it the local accent of some girl from the little town of Sherton, close at hand. " I be tired of waiting, my dear Lord Baxby ! I was afeard you would never come !"

Lady Baxby flushed hot to her toes.

" How the wench loves him!" she said to herself, reasoning from the tones of her voice, which were plaintive and sweet and tender as a bird's. She changed from the home-hating truant to the strategic wife in one moment.

"Hist!" she said.

" My lord, you told me ten o'clock, and 'tis near twelve now," continues the other. " How could ye keep me waiting so if you love me as you said? I should have stuck to my lover in the Parliament troops if it had not been for thee, my dear lord !"

There was not the least doubt that Lady Baxby had been mistaken for her husband by this intriguing damsel. Here was a pretty underhand business ! Here were sly manoeuvrings! Here was faithlessness! Here was a precious assignation surprised in the midst! Her wicked husband, whom till this very moment she had ever deemed the soul of good faith—how could he!

Lady Baxby precipitately retreated to the door in the turret, closed it, locked it, and ascended one round of the staircase, where there was a loop-hole. " I am not coming! I, Lord Baxby, despise ye and all your wanton tribe !" she hissed through the opening; and then crept upstairs, as firmly rooted in Royalist principles as any man in the Castle.

Her husband still slept the sleep of the weary, well-fed, and well-drunken, if not of the just; and Lady Baxby quickly disrobed herself without assistance—being, indeed, supposed by her woman to have retired to rest long ago. Before lying down, she noiselessly locked the door and placed the key under her pillow. More than that, she got a staylace, and, creeping up to her lord, in great stealth tied the lace in a tight knot to one of his long locks of hair, attaching the other end of the lace to the bedpost; for, being tired herself now, she feared she might sleep heavily; and, if her husband should wake, this would be a delicate hint that she had discovered all.

It is added that, to make assurance trebly sure, her gentle ladyship, when she had lain down to rest, held her lord's hand in her own during the whole of the night. But this is old-wives' gossip, and not corroborated. What Lord Baxby thought and said when he awoke the next morning and found himself so strangely tethered, is likewise only matter of conjecture; though there is no reason to suppose that his rage was great. The extent of his culpability as regards the intrigue was this much: that, while halting at a cross-road near Sherton that day, he had flirted with a pretty young woman, who seemed nothing loath, and had invited her to the Castle terrace after dark—an invitation which he quite forgot on his arrival home.

The subsequent relations of Lord and Lady Baxby were not again greatly imbittered by quarrels, so far as is known ; though the husband's conduct in later life was occasionally eccentric, and the vicissitudes of his public career culminated in long exile. The siege of the Castle was not regularly undertaken till two or three years later than the time I have been describing, when Lady Baxby and all the women therein, except the wife of the then governor, had been removed to safe distance. That memorable siege of fifteen days by Fairfax, and the surrender of the old place on an August evening, is matter of history, and need not be told by me.

The man of family spoke approvingly across to the colonel when the Club had done smiling, declaring that the story was an absolutely faithful page of history, as he had good reason to know, his own people having been engaged in that well-known scrimmage. He asked if the colonel had ever heard the equally well-authenticated though less martial tale of a certain Lady Penelope, who lived in the same century, and not a score of miles from the same place ?

The colonel had not heard it, nor had anybody except the local historian; and the inquirer was induced to proceed forthwith.

DAME THE EIGHTH.

Penelope.

BY THE MAN OF FAMILY.

In going out of Casterbridge by the low-lying road which eventually conducts to the town of Ivell, you see on the right hand an ivied manor-house, flanked by battlemented towers, and more than usually distinguished by the size of its many mullioned windows. Though still of good capacity, the building is much reduced from its original grand proportions; it has, moreover, been shorn of the fair estate which once appertained to its lord, with the exception of a few acres of parkland immediately around the mansion. This was formerly the seat of the ancient and knightly family of the Drenghards, or Drenkhards, now extinct in the male line, whose name, according to the local chronicles, was interpreted to mean Strenuus Miles, vel Potator, though certain members of the family were averse to the latter signification, and a duel was fought by one of them on

that account, as is well known. With this, however, we are not now concerned.

In the early part of the reign of the first King James, there was visiting near this place of the Drenghards a lady of noble family and extraordinary beauty. She was of the purest descent; ah, tliere's seldom such blood nowadays as hers! She possessed no great wealth, it was said, but was sufficiently endowed. Her beauty was so perfect, and her manner so entrancing, that suitors seemed to spring out of the ground wherever she went, a sufficient cause of anxiety to the Countess her mother, her only living parent. Of these there were three in particular, whom neither her mother's complaints of prematurity, nor the ready raillery of the maiden herself, could effectually put off. The said gallants were a certain Sir John Gale, a Sir William Hervy, and the well-known Sir George Drenghard, one of the Drenghard family before mentioned. They had, curiously enough, all been equally honored with the distinction of knighthood, and their schemes for seeing her were manifold, each fearing that one of the others would steal a march over himself. Not content with calling, on every imaginable excuse, at the house of the relative with whom she sojourned, they intercepted her in rides and in walks; and if any one of them chanced to surprise another in the act of paying her marked attentions, the encounter often ended in an altercation of great violence. So heated and impassioned, in-

deed, would they become, that the lady hardly felt herself safe in their company at such times, notwithstanding that she was a brave and buxom damsel, not easily put out, and with a daring spirit of humor in her composition, if not of coquetry.

At one of these altercations, which had taken place in her relative's grounds, and was unusually bitter, threatening to result in a duel, she found it necessary to assert herself. Turning haughtily upon the pair of disputants, she declared that whichever should be the first to break the peace between them, no matter what the provocation, that man should never be admitted to her presence again ; and thus would she effectually stultify the aggressor by making the promotion of a quarrel a distinct bar to its object.

While the two knights were wearing rather a crestfallen appearance at her reprimand, the third, never far off, came upon the scene, and she repeated her caveat to him also. Seeing, then, how great was the concern of all at her peremptory mood, the lady's manner softened, as she said, with a roguish smile:

"Have patience, have patience, you foolish men! Only bide your time quietly, and, in faith, I will marry you all in turn!"

They laughed heartily at this sally, all three together, as though they were the best of friends; at which she blushed and showed some embarrassment, not having realized that her arch jest would have sounded so strange when uttered,

The meeting which resulted thus, however, had its good effect in checking the bitterness of their rivahy; and they repeated her speech to their relatives and acquaintance with a hilarious frequency and publicity that the lady little divined, or she might have blushed and felt more embarrassment still.

In the course of time the position resolved itself, and the beauteous Lady Penelope (as she was called) made up her mind, her choice being the eldest of the three knights, Sir George Drenghard, owner of the mansion aforesaid, which thereupon became her home ; and her liusband being a pleasant man, and his family, though not so noble, of as good repute as her own, all things seemed to show that she had reckoned wisely in honoring him with her preference.

But wliat may lie behind the still and silent veil of the future none can foretell. In the course of a few months the husband of her choice died of his convivialities (as if, indeed, to bear out his name), and the Lady Penelope was left alone as mistress of his house. By this time she had apparently quite forgotten her careless declaration to her lovers collectively ; but the lovers tliem-selvcs had not forgotten it; and, as she would now be free to take a second one of them. Sir Joliu Gale appeared at her door as early in the widowhood a8 it was proper and seemly to do so.

She gave him little encouragement; for, of the two remaining, her best beloved was Sir William,

of whom, if the truth must be told, she had often thought during her short married life. But he had not yet reappeared. Her heart began to be so much with him now that she contrived to convey to him, by indirect hints through his friends, that she would not be displeased by a renewal of his former attentions. Sir William, however, misapprehended her gentle signalling, and from excellent though mistaken motives of delicacy, delayed to intrude himself upon her for a long time. Meanwhile Sir John, now created a baronet, was unremitting, and she began to grow somewhat piqued at the backwardness of him she secretly desired to be forward.

" Never mind," her friends said jestingly to her (knowing of her humorous remark, as everybody did, that she would marry them all three if they would have patience)—"never mind ; why hesitate upon the order of them ? Take 'em as they come."

This vexed her still more, and regretting deeply, as she had often done, that such a careless speech should ever have passed her lips, she fairly broke down under Sir John's importunity, and accepted his hand. They were married on a fine spring morning, about the very time at which the unfortunate Sir William discovered her preference for him, and was beginning to hasten home from a foreign court to declare his unaltered devotion to her. On his arrival in England he learned the sad truth.

If Sir William suffered at her precipitancy under what she had deemed his neglect, the Lady-Penelope herself suffered more. She had not long been the wife of Sir John Gale before he showed a disposition to retaliate upon her for the trouble and delay she had put him to in winning her. With increasing frequency he would tell her that, as far as he could perceive, she was an article not worth such labor as he had bestowed in obtaining it, and such snubbings as he had taken from his rivals on the same account. These and other cruel things he repeated till he made the lady weep sorely, and wellnigh broke her spirit, though she had formerly been such a mettlesome dame. By degrees it became perceptible to all her friends that her life was a very unhappy one ; and the fate of the fair woman seemed yet the harder in that it was her own stately mansion, left to her sole use by her first husband, which her second had entered into and was enjoying, his being but a mean and meagre erection.

But such is the flippancy of friends that when she met them, and secretly confided her grief to their ears, they would say, cheerily, " Lord, never mind, my dear ; there's a third to come yet!"—at which maladroit remark she would show much indignation, and tell them they should know better than to trifle on so solemn a theme. Yet that the poor lady would have been only too happy to be the wife of the third, instead of Sir John whom she had taken, was painfully obvious, and much

she was blamed for her foolish choice by some people. Sir William, however, had returned to foreign cities on learning the news of her marriage, and had never been heard of since.

Two or three years of suffering were passed by Lady Penelope as the despised and chidden wife of this man Sir John, amid regrets that she had so greatly mistaken him, and sighs for one whom she thought never to see again, till it chanced that her husband fell sick of some slight ailment. One day after this, when she was sitting in his room, looking from the window upon the expanse in front, she beheld, approaching the house on foot, a form she seemed to know well. Lady Penelope withdrew silently fi-om the sick-room, and descended to the hall, whence, through the door-way, she saw entering between the two round towers, which at that time flanked the gate-way, Sir William Hervy, as she had surmised, but looking thin and travel-worn. She advanced into the courtyard to meet him.

" I was passing through Casterbridge," he said, with faltering deference, " and I walked out to ask after your ladyship's health. I felt that I could do no less; and, of course, to pay my respects to your good husband, ray heretofore acquaintance. . . . But oh, Penelope, th'st look sick and sorry!"

" I am heart-sick, that's all," said she.

They could see in each other an emotion which neither wished to express, and they stood thus a long time with tears in their eyes.

" He does not treat 'ee well, I hear," said Sir William, in a low voice. " May God in heaven forgive him ; but it is asking a great deal!"

" Hush, hush !" said she, hastily.

" Nay, but I will speak what I may honestly say," he answered. "I am not under your roof, and my tongue is free. Why didst not wait for me, Penelope, or send to me a more overt letter ? I would have travelled night and day to come!"

" Too late, William ; you must not ask it," said she, endeavoring to quiet him as in old times. " My husband just now is unwell. He will grow better in a day or two, maybe. You must call again and see him before you leave Casterbridge."

As she said this their eyes met. Each was thinking of her lightsome words about taking the three men in turn ; each thought that two-thirds of that promise had been fulfilled. But, as if it were unpleasant to her that tliis recollection should have arisen, she spoke again quickly: " Come again in a day or two, when my husband will be well enough to see you."

Sir William departed without entering the house, and she returned to Sir John's chamber. He, rising from his pillow, said, "To whom hast been talking, wife, in the court-yard? I heard voices there."

She hesitated, and he repeated the question more impatiently.

" I do not wish to tell you now," said she.

"But I wool! know !" said he. U ..

226 A GROUP OF NOBLE DAMES.

Then she answered, " Sir William Hervy."

"By G—, I thought as much!" cried Sir John, drops of perspiration standing on his white face. "A skulking villain! A sick man's ears are keen, my lady. I heard that they were lover-like tones, and he called 'ee by your Christian name. These be your intrigues, my lady, when I am off my legs a while!"

" On my honor," cried she, " you do me a wrong. I swear I did not know of his coming!"

" Swear as you will," said Sir John, " I don't believe 'ee." And with this he taunted her, and worked himself into a greater passion, which much increased his illness. His lady sat still, brooding. There was that upon her face which had seldom been there since her marriage; and she seemed to think anew of what she had so lightly said in the days of her freedom, when her three lovers were one and all coveting her hand. " I began at the wrong end of ^em," she murmured. " My God—that did I!"

"What?" said he.

" A trifle," said she. " I spoke to myself only."

It was somewhat strange that after this day, while she went about the house with even a sadder face than usual, her churlish husband grew worse; and what was more, to the surprise of all, though to the regret of few, he died a fortnight later. Sir William had not called upon him.as he had promised, having received a private communication from Lady Penelope, frankly informing

him that to do so would be inadvisable, by reason of her husband's temper.

Now when Sir John was gone, and his remains carried to his family burying-place in another part of England, the lady began in due time to wonder whither Sir William had betaken himself. But she had been cured of precipitancy (if ever woman were), and was prepared to wait her whole lifetime a widow if the said Sir William should not reappear. Her life was now passed mostly within the walls, or in promenading between the pleas-aunce and the bowling-green; and she very seldom went even so far as the high-road, which then skirted the grounds on the north, tliough it has now, and for many years, been diverted to the south side. Her patience was rewarded (if love be in any case a reward); for one day, many months after her second husband's death, a messenger arrived at her gate with the intelligence that Sir William Hervy was again in Casterbridge, and would be glad to know if it were her pleasure that he should wait upon her.

It need hardly be said that permission was joyfully granted, and within two hours her lover stood before her, a more thoughtful man than formerly, but in all essential respects the same man, generous, modest to diffidence, and sincere. The reserve which womanly decorum threw over her manner was but too obviously artificial, and when he said "the ways of Providence are strange," and added, after a moment, " and merciful like-

wise," she could not conceal her agitation, and burst into tears upon his neck.

"But this is too soon," she said, starting back.

" But no," said he. " You are eleven months gone in widowhood, and it is not as if Sir John had been a good husband to you."

His visits grew pretty frequent now, as may well be guessed, and in a month or two he began to urge her to an early union. But she counselled a little longer delay.

" Why ?" said he. " Surely I have waited long! Life is short; we are getting older every day, and I am the last of the three."

" Yes," said the lady, frankly. " And that is why I would not have you hasten. Our marriage may seem so strange to everybody, after my unlucky remark on that occasion we know so well, and which so many others know likewise, thanks to tale-bearers."

On this representation he conceded a little space, for the sake of her good name. But the destined day of their marriage at last arrived, and it was a gay time for the villagers and all concerned, and the bells in the parish church rang from noon till night. Thus at last she was united to the man who had loved her the most tenderly of them all, who but for his reticence might perhaps have been the first to win her. Often did he say to himself, " How wondrous that her words should have been fulfilled! Many a truth hath been spoken in jest, but never a more remarkable one!"

The noble lady herself preferred not to dwell on the coincidence, a certain shyness, if not shame, crossing her fair face at any allusion thereto.

But people will have their say, sensitive souls or none, and their sayings on this third occasion took a singular shape. " Surely," they whispered, " there is something more than chance in this. . . . The death of the first was possibly natural; but what of the death of the second, who ill-used her, and whom, loving the third so desperately, she must have wished out of the way!"

Then they pieced together sundry trivial incidents of Sir John's illness, and dwelt upon the indubitable truth that he had grown worse after her lover's unexpected visit; till a very sinister theory was built up as to the hand she may have had in Sir John's premature demise. But nothing of this suspicion was said openly, for she was a lady of noble birth—nobler, indeed, than either of her husbands—and what people suspected they feared to express in formal accusation.

The mansion that she occupied had been left to her for so long a time as she should choose to reside in it, and, having a regard for the spot, she had coaxed Sir William to remain there. But in the end it was unfortunate; for one day, when in the full tide of his happiness, he was walking among the willows near the gardens, where he overheard a conversation between some basket-makers who were cutting the osiers for their use. In this fatal dialogue the suspicions of the neighboring townsfolk were revealed to him for the first time.

" A cupboard close to his bed, and the key in her pocket. Ah!" said one.

"And a blue phial therein—h'm!" said another.

"And spurge - laurel leaves among the hearth-ashes. Oh-oh!" said a third.

On his return home Sir William seemed to have aged years. But he said nothing; indeed, it was a thing impossible. And from that hour a ghastly estrangement began. She could not understand it, and simply waited. One day he said, however, " I must go abroad."

" Why ?" said she. " William, have I offended you ?"

" No," said he; " but I must go."

She could coax little more out of him, and in itself there was nothing unnatural in his departure, for he had been a wanderer from his youth. In a few days he started off, apparently quite another man than he who had rushed to her side so devotedly a few months before.

It is not known when, or how, the rumors, which were so thick in the atmosphere around her, actually reached the Lady Penelope's ears, but that they did reach her there is no doubt. It was impossible that they should not; the district teemed with them; they rustled in the air like night birds of evil omen. Then a reason for her husband's departure occurred to her appalled mind, and a loss of health became quickly apparent. She dwindled thin in the face, and the veins in her temples could all be distinctly traced. An inner fire seemed to be withering her away. Her rings fell off her fingers, and her arms hung like the flails of the threshers, though they had till lately been so round and so elastic. She wrote to her husband repeatedly, begging him to return to her; but he, being in extreme and wretched doubt—moreover, knowing nothing of her ill-health, and never suspecting that the rumors had reached her also—deemed absence best, and postponed his return a while, giving various good reasons for his delay.

At length, however, when the Lady Penelope had given birth to a still-born child, her mother, the Countess, addressed a letter to Sir William, requesting him to come back to her if he wished to see her alive; since she was wasting away of some mysterious disease, which seemed to be rather mental than physical. It was evident that his mothei'-in-law knew nothing of the secret, for she lived at a distance; but Sir William promptly hastened home, and stood beside the bed of his now dying wife.

"Believe me, William," she said, when they were alone, "I am innocent—innocent!"

"Of what?" said he. "Heaven forbid that I should accuse you of anything!"

"But you do accuse me—silently!" she gasped. " I could not write thereon—and ask you to hear me. It was too much, too degrading. But would that I had been less proud! They suspect me of poisoning hira, William! But, oh my dear husband, I am innocent of that wicked crime! He died naturally. I loved you—too soon; but that was all!"

Nothing availed to save her. The worm had gnawed too far into her heart before Sir William's return for anything to be remedial now; and in a few weeks she breathed her last. After her death the people spoke louder, and her conduct became a subject of public discussion. A little later on, the physician who had attended the late Sir John heard the rumor, and came down from the place near London to which he latterly had retired, with the express purpose of calling upon Sir William Hervy, now staying in Casterbridge.

He stated that, at the request of a relative of Sir John's, who wished to be assured on the matter by reason of its suddenness, he had, with the assistance of a surgeon, made a private examination of Sir John's body immediately after his decease, and found that it had resulted from purely natural causes. Nobody at this time had breathed a suspicion of foul play, and therefore nothing was said which might afterwards have established her innocence.

It being thus placed beyond doubt that this beautiful and noble lady had been done to death by a vile scandal that was wholly unfounded, her husband was stung with a dreadful remorse at the share he had taken in her misfortunes, and left

the country anew, this time never to return alive. He survived her but a few years, and his body was brought home and buried beside his wife's under the tomb which is still visible in the i)arish church. Until lately there was a good portrait of her, in weeds for her first husband, with a cross in her hand, at the ancestral seat of her family, where she was much pitied, as she deserved to be. Yet there were some severe enough to say—and these not unjust persons in other respects—that though unquestionably innocent of the crime imputed to her, she had shown an unseemly wantonness in contracting three marriages in such rapid succession; that the untrue suspicion might have been ordered by Providence (who often works indirectly) as a punishment for her self-indulgence. Upon that point I have no opinion to offer.

The reverend the vice-president, however, the tale being ended, offered as his opinion that her fate ought to be quite clearly recognized as a punishment. So thought the church-warden, and also the quiet gentleman sitting near. The latter knew many other instances in point, one of which could be narrated in a few words.

DAME THE NINTH.

Ube JHucbess of UDamptonsblre,

BY THE QUIET GENTLEMAN.

Some fifty years ago, the then Duke of Hamp-tonshire, fifth of that title, was incontestably the head man in his county, and particularly in the neighborhood of Batton. He came of the ancient and loyal family of Saxelbye, which, before its ennoblement, had numbered many knightly and ecclesiastical celebrities in its male line. It would have occupied a painstaking county historian a whole afternoon to take rubbings of the numerous eflSgies and heraldic devices graven to their memory on the brasses, tablets, and altar-tombs in the aisle of the parish church. The Duke himself, however, was a man little attracted by ancient chronicles in stone and metal, even when they concerned his own beginnings. He allowed his mind to linger by preference on the many graceless and unedifying pleasures which his position placed at his command. He could on oc-

casion close the mouths of his dependants by a good bomb-like oath, and he argued doggedly with the parson on the virtues of cock-fighting and baiting the bull.

This nobleman's personal appearance was somewhat impressive. His complexion was that of the copperbeech-tree. His frame was stalwart, though slightly stoojnng. His mouth was large, and he carried an unpolished sapling as his walking-stick, except when he carried a spud for cutting up any thistle he encountered on his walks. His castle stood in the midst of a park, surrounded by dusky elms, except to the southward; and when the moon shone out, the gleaming stone fa5ade, backed by heavy boughs, was visible from the distant high-road as a white spot on the surface of darkness. Though called a castle, the building was little forti6ed, and had been erected witli greater eye to internal convenience than those crannied places of defence to which the name strictly appertains. It was a castellated mansion as regular as a chess-board on its ground-plan, ornamented with make-believe bastions and machicolations, behind which were stacks of battlemented chimneys. On still mornings, at the fire-lighting hour, when ghostly housemaids stalk the corridors, and thin streaks of light through the shutter-chinks lend startling winks and smiles to ancestors on canvas, twelve or fifteen thin stems of blue smoke sprouted upward from these chimney-tops, and spread into a flat canopy on high. Around the site stretched 10,000 acres of good, fat, unimpeachable soil, plentiful in glades and lawns wherever visible from the castle-windows, and merging in homely arable where screened from the too-curious eye by ingeniously-contrived plantations.

Some way behind the owner of all this came the second man in the parish, the rector, the Honorable and Reverend Mr. Oldbourne, a widower, over stiff and stern for a clergyman, whose severe white neckcloth, well-kept gray hair, and right-lined face betokened none of those sympathetic traits whereon depends so much of a parson's power to do good among his fellow-creatures. The last, far-removed man of the series — altogether the Neptune of these local primaries—was the curate, Mr. Alwyn Hill. He was a handsome young deacon, with curly hair, dreamy eyes—so dreamy that to look long into them was like ascending and floating among summer clouds — a complexion as fresh as a flower, and a chin absolutely beardless. Though his age was about twenty-five, he looked not much over nineteen.

The rector had a daughter called Emmeline, of so sweet and simple a nature that her beauty was discovered, measured, and inventoried by almost everybody in that part of the country before it was suspected by herself to exist. She had been bred in comparative solitude; a rencounter with men ti'oubled and confused her. Whenever a strange visitor came to her father's house she slipped into the orchard and remained till he was gone, ridiculing her weakness in apostrophes, but unable to overcome it. Her virtues lay in no resistant force of character, but in a natural inap-petency for evil things, which to her were as unmeaning as joints of flesh to a herbivorous creature. Iler charms of person, manner, and mind had been clear for some time to the Antinous in orders, and no less so to the Duke, who, though scandalously ignorant of dainty phrases, ever showing a clumsy manner towards the gentle sex, and, in short, not at all a lady's man, took fire to a degree that was wellnigh terrible at sudden sight of Emmeline, a short time after she was turned seventeen.

It occurred one afternoon at the corner of a shrubbery between the castle and the rectory, where the Duke was standing to watch the heaving of a mole, when the fair girl brushed past at a distance of a few yards, in the full light of the sun, and without hat or bonnet. The Duke went home like a man who had seen a spirit. He ascended to the picture-gallery of his castle, and there passed some time in staring at the by-gone beauties of his lino as if he had never before considered what an important part those specimens of womankind had played in the evolution of the Saxelbye race. He dined alone, drank rather freely, and declared to himself that Emmeline Oldbourne must be his.

Meanwhile there had, unfortunately, arisen between the curate and this girl some sweet and secret understanding. Particulars of the attach-ment remained unknown then and always, but it was plainly not approved of by her father. His procedure was cold, hard, and inexorable. Soon the curate disappeared from the parish, almost suddenly, after bitter and hard words had been heard to pass between him and the rector one evening in the garden, intermingled with which, like the cries of the dying in the din of battle, were the beseeching sobs of a woman. Not long after this it was announced that a marriage be-tween the Duke and Miss Oldbourne was to be solemnized at a surprisingly early date.

The wedding-day came and passed; and she was a duchess. Nobody seemed to think of the ousted man during the day, or else those who thought of him concealed their meditations. Some of the less subservient ones were disposed to speak in a jocular manner of the august husband and wife, others to make correct and pretty speeches about them, according as their sex and nature dictated. But in the evening, the ringers in the belfry, with whom Alwyn had been a favorite, eased their minds a little concerning the gentle young man, and the possible regrets of the woman he had loved.

"Don't you see something wrong in it all?" said the third bell, as he wiped his face. "I know well enough where she would have liked to stable her horses to-night, when they have done their journey."

" That is, you would know if you could tell where young Mr, Hill is living, which is known to none in the parish."

" Except to the lady that this ring o' grandsire triples is in honor of."

Yet these friendly cottagers were at this time far from suspecting the real dimensions of Emme-line's misery, nor was it clear even to those who came into much closer communion with her than they, so well had she concealed her heart-sickness. But bride and bridegroom had not long been home at the castle when the young wife's unhap-piness became plainly enough perceptible. Her maids and men said that she was in the habit of turning to the wainscot and shedding stupid, scalding tears at a time when a right-minded lady would have been overhauling her wardrobe. She prayed earnestly in the great church-pew, where she sat lonely and insignificant as a mouse in a cell, instead of counting her rings, falling asleep, or amusing herself in silent laughter at the queer old people in the congregation, as previous beauties of the family had done in their time. She seemed to care no more for eating and drinking out of crystal and silver than from a service of earthen vessels. Her head was, in truth, full of something else; and that such was the case was only too obvious to the Duke, her husband. At first he would only taunt her for her folly in think-, ing of that milk-and-water parson ; but as time went on his charges took a more positive shape. He would not believe her assurance that she had in

no way communicated witli her former lover, nor he with her, since their parting in the presence of her father. This led to some strange scenes between them which need not be detailed; their result was soon to take a catastrophic shape.

One dark, quiet evening, about two months after the marriage, a man entered the gate admitting from the highway to the park and avenue which ran up to the house. He arrived within two hundred yards of the walls, when he left the gravelled drive and drew near to the castle by a roundabout path leading into a shrubbery. Here he stood still. In a few minutes the strokes of the castle-clock resounded, and then a female figure entered the same secluded nook from an opposite direction. There the two indistinct persons leaped together like a pair of dewdrops on a leaf; and then they stood apart, facing each other, the woman looking down.

" Emmeline, you begged me to come, and here I am, Heaven forgive me!" said the man, hoarsely.

" You are going to emigrate, Alwyn," she said, in broken accents. " I have heard of it; you sail from Plymouth in three days in the Western Glory P'

" Yes. I can live in England no longer. Life is as death to me here," says he.

" My life is even worse — worse than death. Death would not have driven me to this extremity. Listen, Alwyn — I have sent for you to beg to go with you, or at least to be near you—to do anything so that it be not to stay here."

" To go away with me ?" he said, in a startled tone.

" Yes, yes—or under your direction, or by your help in some way! Don't be horrified at me— you must bear with me while I implore it. Nothing short of cruelty Avould have driven me to this. I could have borne ray doom in silence had I been left unmolested; but he tortures me, and I shall soon be in the grave if I cannot escape."

To his shocked inquiry how her husband tortured her, the Duchess said that it was by jealousy. " He tries to wring admissions from me concerning you," she said, " and will not believe that I have not communicated with you since my engagement to him was settled by my father, and I was forced to agree to it."

The poor curate said that this was the heaviest news of all. " lie has not personally ill-used you ?" he asked.

" Yes," she whispered.

" What has he done ?"

She looked fearfully around, and said, sobbing : "In trying to make me confess to what I have never done, he adopts plans I dare not describe for terrifying me into a weak state, so that I may own to anything ! I resolved to write to you, as I liad no other friend." She added, with dreary irony," I thought I would give him some ground for his susi»icion, so as not to disgrace his judgment." 16

"Do you really mean, Emmeline," lie tremblingly inquired, " that you—that you want to fly with me?"

" Can you think that I would act otherwise than in earnest at such a time at this ?"

He was silent for a minute or more. "You must not go with me," he said.

"Why?"

"It would be sin."

" It cannot be sin, for I have never wanted to commit sin in my life; and it isn't likely I would begin now, when I pray every day to die and be sent to Heaven out of my misery!"

"But it is wrong, Emmeline, all the same."

" Is it wrong to run away from the fire that scorches you ?"

" It would look wrong, at any rate, in this case."

"Alwyn, Alwyn, take me, I beseech you!" she burst out. " It is not right in general, I know, but it is such an exceptional instance, this. Why has such a sevei^e strain been put upon me ? I was doing no harm, injuring no one, helping many people, and expecting happiness; yet trouble came. Can it be that God holds me in derision? I had no supporter—I gave way; and now raj life is a burden and a shame to me, . . . Oh, if you only knew how much to me this request to you is— how my life is wrapped up in it, you could not deny me!"

" This is almost beyond endurance — Heaven support US," he groaned. "Emmy, you are the Duchess of Hamptonshire, the Duke of Hampton-shire's wife; you must not go witli me!"

"And am I then refused ?—Oh, am I refused ?" she ci-ied, frantically. "Alwyn, Alwyn, do you say it indeed to me ?"

"Yes, I do, dear, tender heart! I do most sadly say it. You must not go. Forgive me, for there is no alternative but refusal. Though I die, though you die, we must not fly together. It is forbidden in God's law. Good-bye, for always and ever!"

He tore himself away, hastened from the shrubbery, and vanished among the trees.

Three days after this meeting and farewell, Alwyn, his soft, handsome features stamped with a haggard hardness that ten years of ordinary wear and tear in the world could scarcely have produced, sailed from Plymouth on a drizzling morning, in the passenger-ship Westerti Glory. When the land had faded behind him he mechanically endeavored to school himself into a stoical frame of mind. His attempt, backed up by the strong moral staying-power that had enabled him to resist the passionate temptation to which Em-meline, in her reckless trustfulness, had exposed him, was rewarded by a certain kind of success, though the murmuring stretch of waters whereon he gazed day after day too often seemed to be articulating to him in tones of her well-remembered voice.

He framed on his journey rules of conduct for reducing to mild proportions the feverish regrets which would occasionally arise and agitate him, when he indulged in visions of what might have been had he not hearkened to the whispers of conscience. He fixed his thoughts for so many hours a day on philosophical passages in the volumes he had brought with him, allowing himself now and then a few minutes' thought of Emmeline, with the strict yet reluctant niggardliness of an ailing epicure proportioning the rank drinks that cause his malady. The voyage was marked by the usual incidents of a sailing-passage in those days—a storm, a calm, a man overboard, a birth, and a funeral—the latter sad event being one in which he, as the only clergyman on board, officiated, reading the service ordained for the purpose. The ship duly arrived at Boston early in the month following, and thence he proceeded to Providence to seek out a distant relative.

After a short stay at Providence he returned again to Boston, and by applying himself to a serious occupation made good progress in shaking off the dreary melancholy which enveloped him even now. Distracted and weakened in his beliefs by his recent experiences, he decided that he could not for a time worthily fill the office of a minister of religion, and applied for the mastership of a school. Some introductions, given him before starting, were useful now, and he soon became known as a respectable scholar and gentle-man to the trustees of one of the colleges. This ultimately led to his retirement from the school and installation in the college as professor of rhetoric and oratory.

Here and thus he lived on, exerting himself solely because of a conscientious determination to do his duty. He passed his winter evenings in turning sonnets and elegies, often giving his thoucrhts voice in "Lines to an Unfortunate Lady," -while his summer leisure at the same hour would be spent in watching the lengthening shadows from his window, and fancifully comparing them with the shades of his own life. If he walked, he mentally inquired which was the eastern quarter of the landscape, and thought of the 2000 miles of water that way, and of what was beyond it. In a Avord, he was at all spare times dreaming of her who was only a memory to him, and would probably never be more.

Nine years passed by, and under their wear and tear Alwyn Hill's face lost a great many of the attractive characteristics which had formerly distinguished it. He was kind to his pupils and affable to all who came in contact with him; but the kernel of his life, his secret, was kept as snugly shut up as though he had been dumb. In talking to his acquaintances of England and his life there, he omitted the episode of Batton Castle and Emmeline as if it had no existence in his calendar at all. Though of towering importance to himself, it had filled but a short and small fragment of time, an ephemeral season which would have been wellnigh imperceptible, even to him, at this distance, but for the incident it enshrined.

One day, at this date, when cursorily glancing over an old English newspaper, he observed a paragraph which, short as it was, contained for him whole tomes of thrilling information—rung with more passion-stirring rhythm than the collected cantos of all the poets. It was an announcement of the death of the Duke of Hamp-tonshire, leaving behind him a widow, but no children.

The current of Alwyn's thoughts now completely changed. On looking again at the newspaper he found it to be one that was sent him long ago, and had been carelessly thrown aside. But for an accidental overhauling of the waste journals in his study he might not have known of the event for years. At this moment of reading the Duke had already been dead seven months. Alwyn could now no longer bind himself down to machine-made synecdoche, antithesis, and climax, being full of spontaneous specimens of all these rhetorical forms, which he dared not utter. Who shall wonder that his mind luxuriated in dreams of a sweet possibility now laid open for the first time these many years? for Emmeline was to him now as ever the one dear thing in all the world. The issue of his silent romancing was that he resolved to return to her at the very earliest moment.

But he could not abandon his professional work on the instant. He did not get really quite free from engagements till four months later; but, though suffering throes of impatience continually, he said to himself every day : " If she has continued to love me nine years she will love me ten; she will think the more tenderly of me when her present hours of solitude shall have done their proper work; old times will revive with the cessation of her recent experience, and every day will favor my return."

The enforced interval soon passed, and he duly arrived in England, reaching the village of Bat-ton on a certain winter day between twelve and thirteen months subsequent to the time of the Duke's death.

It was evening; yet such was Alwyn's impatience that he could not forbear taking, this very night, one look at the castle which Emmeline had entered as unhappy mistress ten years before. He threaded the park trees, gazed in passing at well-known outlines which rose against the dim sky, and was soon interested in observing that lively country-people, in parties of two and three, were walking before and behind him up the interlaced avenue to the castle gate-way. Knowing himself to be safe from recognition, Alwyn inquired of one of these pedestrians what was going on.

"Her Grace gives her tenantry a ball to-night, to keep up the old custom of the Duke and his father before him, which she does not wish to change."

" Indeed! Has she lived here entirely alone since the Duke's death'?"

" Quite alone. But though she doesn't receive company herself, she likes the village people to enjoy themselves, and often has 'em here."

"Kind-hearted, as always!" thought Alwyn.

On reaching the castle he found that the great gates at the tradesmen's entrance were thrown back against the wall as if they were never to be closed again; that the passages and rooms in that wing were brilliantly lighted up, some of the numerous candles guttering down over the green leaves which decorated them, and upon the silk dresses of the happy farmers' wives as they passed beneath, each on her husband's arm. Alwyn found no difficulty in marching in along with the rest, the castle being Liberty Hall tonight. He stood unobserved in a corner of the large apartment where dancing was about to begin.

" Her Grace, though hardly out of mourning, will be sure to come down and lead off the dance with neighbor Bates," said one.

"Who is neighbor Bates?" asked Alwyn.

"An old man she respects much—the oldest of her tenant-farmers. He was seventy-eight his last birthday."

"Ah, to be sure!" said Alwyn, at his ease. " I remember."

The dancers formed in line, and waited. A door opened at the farther end of the hall, and a lady in black silk came forth. She bowed, smiled, and proceeded to the top of the dance.

"Who is that lady?" said Alwyn, in a puzzled tone. "I thought you told me that the Duchess of Hamptonshire—"

" That is the Duchess," said his informant.

" But there is another ?"

" No; there is no other."

"But she is not the Duchess of Hamptonshire —who used to—" Alwyn's tongue stuck to his mouth, he could get no further.

"What's the matter?" said his acquaintance. Alwyn had retired, and was supporting himself against the wall.

The wretched Alwyn murmured something about a stitch in his side from walking. Then the music struck up, the dance went on, and his neighbor became so interested in watching the movements of this strange duchess through its mazes as to forget Alwjm for a while.

It gave him an opportunity to brace himself up. He was a man who had suffered, and he could suffer again. " IIow came that person to be your duchess?" he asked, in a firm, distinct voice, when he had attained complete self-command. *' Where is her other Grace of Hamptonshire? There certainly was another. I know it."

"Oh, the previous one! Yes, yes. She ran away years and years ago with the young curate. Mr. Hill was the young man's name, if I recollect."

*' No! She never did. What do you mean by that?" he said.

"Yes, she certainly ran away. She met the curate in the shrubbery about a couple of months after her marriage with the Duke. There were folks who saw the meeting and heard some words of their talk. They arranged to go, and she sailed from Plymouth with him a day or two afterwards."

" That's not true."

" Then 'tis the queerest lie ever told by man. Her father believed and knew to his dying day that she went with him; and so did the Duke, and everybody about here. Aye, there was a fine upset about it at the time. The Duke traced her to Plymouth."

"Traced her to Plymouth?"

"He traced her to Plymouth, and set on his spies; and they found that she went to the shipping-office, and inquired if Mr. Alwyn Hill had entered his name as passenger by the Wester?i Glory; and when she found that he had, she booked herself for the same ship, but not in her real name. When the vessel had sailed a letter reached the Duke from her, telling him what she had done. She never came back here again. His Grace lived by himself a number of years, and married this lady only twelve months before he died."

Alwyn was in a state of indescribable bewilderment. But, unmanned as he was, he called the next day on the, to him, spurious Duchess of Hamptonshire. At first she was alarmed at his statement, then cold, then she was won over by his condition to give confidence for confidence. She showed him a letter which had been found among the papers of the late Duke, corroborating what Alwyn's informant had detailed. It was from Emmeline, bearing the postmarked date at which the Western Glory sailed, and briefly stated that she had emigrated by that ship to America.

Alwyn applied himself body and mind to unravel the remainder of the mystery. The story repeated to him was always the same: " She ran away with the curate." A strangely circumstantial piece of intelligence was added to this when he had pushed his inquiries a little further. There was given him the name of a waterman at Plymouth, who had come forward at the time that she was missed and sought for by her husband, and had stated that he put her on board the Wester7i Glory at dusk one evening before that vessel sailed.

After several days of search about the alleys and quays of Plymouth Barbican, during which these impossible words, "She ran off with the curate," became branded on his brain, Alwyn found this important waterman. lie was positive as to the truth of his story, still remembering the incident well, and he described in detail the lady's dress, as he had long ago described it to her husband, which description corresponded
in every particular with the dress worn by Em-meline on the evening of their parting.

Before proceeding to the other side of the Atlantic to continue his inquiries there, the puzzled and distracted Alwyn set himself to ascertain the address of Captain Wheeler, who had commanded the Western Glory in the year of Alwyn's voyage out, and immediately wrote a letter to him on the subject.

The only circumstances which the sailor could recollect or discover from his papers in connection with such a story were, that a woman bearing the name which Alwyn had mentioned as fictitious certainly did come aboard for a voyage he made about that time; that she took a common berth among the poorest emigrants; that she died on the voyage out, at about five days' sail from Plymouth; that she seemed a lady in manners and education. Why she had not applied for a first-class passage, why she had no trunks, they could not guess, for though she had little money in her pocket she had that about her which would have fetched it. " We buried her at sea," continued the captain. "A young parson, one of the cabin-passengers, read the burial-service over her, I remember well."

The whole scene and proceedings darted upon Alwyn's recollection in a moment. It was a fine breezy morning on that long-past voyage out, and he had been told that they were running at the rate of a hundred and odd miles a day. The news went round that one of the poor young women in the other part of the vessel was ill of fever, and delirious. The tidings caused no little alarm among the passengers, for the sanitary conditions of the ship were anything but satisfactory. Shortly after this the doctor announced that she had died. Then Ahvyn had learned that she was laid out for burial in great haste, because of the danger that would have been incurred by delay. And next the funeral scene rose before him, and the prominent part that he had taken in that solemn ceremony. The captain had come to him, requesting him to officiate, as there was no chaplain on board. This he had agreed to do; and as the sun went down with a blaze in his face, he read amid them all assembled: " We therefore commit her body to the deep, to be turned into corruption, looking for the resurrection of the body when the sea shall give up her dead."

The captain also forwarded the addresses of the ship's matron and of other persons who had been engaged on board at the date. To these Alwyn went in the course of time. A categorical description of the clothes of the dead truant, the color of her hair, and other things, extinguished forever all hope of a mistake in identity.

At last, then, the course of events had become clear. On that unhappy evening when he left Emmeline in the shrubbery, forbidding her to follow him because it would be a sin, she must have disobeyed. She must have followed at his

heels silently through the darkness, like a poor pet animal that will not be driven back. She could have accumulated nothing for the journey more than she might have carried in her hand; and thus poorly provided she must have embarked. Her intention had doubtless been to make her presence on board known to him as soon as she could muster courage to do so.

Thus the ten years' chapter of Alwyn Hill's romance wound itself up under his eyes. That the poor young woman in the steerage had been the young Duchess of Hamptonshire was never publicly disclosed. Hill had no longer any reason for remaining in England, and soon after left its shores with no intention to return. Previous to his departure he confided his story to an old friend from his native town—grandfather of the person who now relates it to you.

A few members, including the bookworm, seemed to be impressed by the quiet gentleman's tale; but the member we have called the Spark—who, by the way, was getting somewhat tinged with the light of other days, and owned to eight-and-thirty, and who walked daintily about the room instead of sitting down by the fire with the majority, and said that, for his part, he preferred something more lively than the last story—something in which such long-separated lovers were ultimately united. He also liked stories that were

more modern in their date of action than those he had heard to-day.

Members immediately requested him to give them a specimen, to which the Spark replied that he didn't mind, as far as that went. And though the vice-president, the man of family, the colonel, and others, looked at their watches, and said they must soon retire to their respective quarters in the hotel adjoining, they all decided to sit out the Spark's story.

DAME THE TENTH.
Ube Ibonorable Xaura.
BY THE SPARK.

It was a cold and gloomy. Christmas Eve. The mass of cloud overhead was almost impervious to such daylight as still lingered on; the snow lay several inches deep upon the ground, and the slanting downfall which still went on threatened to considerably increase its thickness before the morning. The Prospect Hotel, a building standing near the wild north coast of Lower Wessex, looked so lonely and so useless at such a time as this that a passing wayfarer would have been led to forget summer possibilities, and to wonder at the commercial courage which could invest capital, on the basis of the popular taste for the picturesque, in a country subject to such dreary phases. That the district was alive with visitors in August seemed but a dim tradition in weather so totally opposed to all that tempts mankind from home. However, there the hotel

stood immovable; and the cliffs, creeks, and headlands which were the primary attractions of the spot, rising in full view on the opposite side of the valley, were now but stern, angular outlines, while the townlet in front was tinged over with a grimy dirtiness rather than the pearly gray that in summer lent such beauty to its appearance.

Within the hotel commanding this outlook the landlord walked idly about with his hands in hia pockets, not in the least expectant of a visitor, and yet unable to settle down to any occupation which should compensate in some degree for the losses that winter idleness entailed on his regular profession. So little, indeed, was anybody expected, that the coffee-room waiter—a genteel boy, whose plated buttons in summer were as close together upon the front of his short jacket as peas in a pod—now appeared in the back yard, metamorphosed into the unrecognizable shape of a rough country lad in corduroys and hobnailed boots, sweeping the snow away, and talking the local dialect in all its purity, quite oblivious of the new polite accent he had learned in the hot weather from the well-behaved visitors. The front door was closed, and, as if to express still more fully the sealed and chrysalis state of the establishment, a sand-bag was placed at the bottom to keep out the insidious snow-drift, the wind setting in directly from that (juarter.

The landlord, entering his own parlor, walked 17
to the large fire which it was absolutely necessary to keep up for his comfort, no such blaze burning in the coffee-room or elsewhere, and, after giving it a stir, returned to a table in the lobby, whereon lay the visitors' book—now closed and pushed back against the wall. He carelessly opened it; not a name had been entered there since the 19th of the previous November, and that was only the name of a man who had arrived on a tricycle, who, indeed, had not been asked to enter at all.

While he was engaged thus the evening grew darker; but before it was yet too dark to distinguish objects upon the road winding round the back of the cliffs, the landlord perceived a black spot on the distant white, which speedily enlarged itself and drew near. The probabilities were that this vehicle—for a vehicle of some sort it seemed to be—would pass by and pursue its way to the nearest rail way - to wn, as others had done. But, contrary to the landlord's expectation, as he stood conning it through the yet unshuttered windows, the solitary object, on reaching the corner, turned into the hotel-front, and drove up to the door.

It was a conveyance particularly unsuited to such a season and weather, being nothing more substantial than an open basket-carriage drawn by a single horse. Within sat two persons, of different sexes, as could soon be discerned, in spite of their muffled attire. The man held the reins, and the lady had got some shelter froni the storm
by clinging close to his side. The landlord rang the hostler's bell to attract the attention of the stable-man, for the approach of the visitors had been deadened to noiselessness by the snow, and when the hostler had come to the horse's liead the gentleman and lady alighted, the landlord meeting them in the hall.

The male stranger was a foreign-looking individual of about eight-and-twenty. lie was close shaven, excepting a mustache, his features being good and even handsome. The lady, Avho stood timidly behind him, seemed to be much younger —possibly not more than eighteen, though it was difficult to judge either of her age or appearance in her present wrappings.

The gentleman expressed his wish to stay till the morning, explaining somewhat unnecessarily, considering that the house was an inn, that they had been unexpectedly benighted on their drive. Such a welcome being given them as landlords can give in dull times, the latter ordered fires in the drawing and coffee rooms, and went to the boy in the yard, who soon scrubbed himself up, dragged his disused jacket from its box, polished the buttons with his sleeve, and appeared civilized in the hall. The lady was shown into a room where she could take off her snow-damped garments, which she sent down to be dried, her companion, meanwhile, putting a couple of sovereigns on the table, as if anxious to make everything smooth and comfortable at starting, and request-

ing that a private sitting-room might be got ready. The landlord assured him that the best up-stairs parlor—usually public—should be kept private this evening, and sent the maid to light the candles. Dinner was prepared for them, and, at the gentleman's desire, served in the same apartment, where, the young lady having joined him, they were left to the rest and refreshment they seemed to need.

That something was peculiar in the relations of the pair had more than once struck the landlord, though wherein that peculiarity lay it was hard to decide. But that his guest was one who paid his way readily had been proved by his conduct, and, dismissing conjectures, he turned to practical affairs.

About nine o'clock he re-entered the hall, and, everything being done for the day, again walked up and down, occasionally gazing through the glass door at the prospect without, to ascertain how the weather was progressing. Contrary to prognostication, snow had ceased falling, and, with the rising of the moon, the sky had partially cleared, light fleeces of cloud drifting across the silvery disk. There was every sign that a frost was going to set in later on. For these reasons the distant rising road was even more distinct now between its high banks than it had been in the declining daylight. Not a track or rut broke the virgin surface of the white mantle that lay along it, all marks left by the lately-arrived travellers having been speedily obliterated by the flakes falling at the time.

And now the landlord beheld by the light of the moon a sight very similar to that he had seen by the light of day. Again a black Bpot was advancing down the road that margined the coast. lie was in a moment or two enabled to perceive that the present vehicle moved onward at a more headlong \'7d)ace than the little carriage which had preceded it; next, that it was a brougham drawn by two powerful horses; next, that this carriage, like the former one, was bound for the hotel door. This desirable feature of resemblance caused the landlord to once more withdraw the sand-bag and advance into the porch.

An old gentleman was the first to alight. He was followed by a young one, and both unhesitatingly came forward.

" Has a young lady, less than nineteen years of age, recently arrived here in the company of a man some years her senior?" asked the old gentleman, in haste. "A man cleanly shaven for the most part, having the appearance of an opera-singer, and calling himself Signor Smithozzi?"

" We have had arrivals lately," said the landlord, in the tone of having had twenty at least— not caring to acknowledge the attenuated state of business that afflicted Prospect Hotel in winter.

"And among them can your memory recall two such as those I describe—the man a sort of barytone ?"

" There certainly is or was a young couple staying in the hotel; but I could not pronounce on the compass of the gentleman's voice,"

" No, no; of course not. I am quite bewildered. They arrived in a basket-carriage, altogether badly provided?"

" They came in a carriage, I believe, as most of our visitors do."

" Yes, yes. I must see them at once. Pardon my want of ceremony, and show us in to where they are."

"But, sir, you forget. Suppose the lady and gentleman I mean are not the lady and gentleman you mean? It would be awkward to allow you to rush in upon them just now while they are at dinner, and might cause me to lose their future patronage."

" True, true. They may not be the same persons. My anxiety, I perceive, makes me rash in my assumptions !"

"Upon the whole, I think they must be the same, Uncle Quantock," said the young man, who had not till now spoken. And turning to the landlord: " You possibly have not such a large assemblage of visitors here, on this somewhat forbidding evening, that you quite forget how this couple arrived and what the lady wore?" His tone of addressing the landlord had in it a quiet frigidity that was not without irony.

" Ah, what she wore; that's it, James. "What did she wear ?"

" I don't usually take stock of my guests' clothing," replied the landlord, dryly, for the ready money of the first arrival had decidedly biassed him in favor of that gentleman's cause. " You can certainly see some of it if you want to," he added, carelessly, "for it is drying by the kitchen fire."

Before the words were half out of his mouth the old gentleman had exclaimed, "Ah!" and precipitated himself along what seemed to be the passage to the kitchen ; but as this turned out to be only the entrance to a dark china closet, he hastily emerged again, after a collision with the inn crockery had told him of his mistake.

" I beg your pardon, I'm sure; but if you only knew my feelings (which I cannot at present explain), you would make allowances. Anything I have broken I will willingly pay for."

"Don't mention it, sir,"said the landlord. And showing the way, they adjourned to the kitchen without further parley. The eldest of the party instantly seized the lady's cloak, that hung upon a clothes-horse, exclaiming : "Ah, yes, James, it is hers ! I knew we were on their track."

" Yes, it is hers," answered the nephew, quietly, for he was much less excited than his companion.

" Show us their room at once," said the old man.

"William, have the lady and gentleman in the front sitting-room finished dining?"

"Yes, sir, long ago," said the hundred plated buttons.

"Then show up these gentlemen to them at once. You stay here to-night, gentlemen, I presume ? Shall the horses be taken out ?"

" Feed the horses and wash their mouths. Whether we stay or not depends upon circumstances," said the placid young man, as he followed his uncle and the waiter to the staircase.

" I think, Nephew James," said the former, as he paused with his foot on the first step—"I think we had better not be announced, but take them by surprise. She may go throwing herself out of the window, or do some equally desperate thing!"

" Yes, certainly, we'll enter unannounced." And he called back the lad who preceded them.

" I cannot sufficiently thank you, James, for so effectually aiding me in this pursuit!" exclaimed the old gentleman, taking the other by the hand. " My increasing infirmities would have hindered my overtaking her to-night, had it not been for your timely aid."

"I am only too happy, uncle, to have been of service to you in this or any other matter. I only wish I could have accompanied you on a pleas-anter journey. However, it is advisable to go up to them at once, or they may hear us." And they softly ascended the stairs.

On the door being opened, a room too large to be comfortable, lit by the best branch-candlesticks of the hotel, was disclosed, before the fire of which apartment the truant couple were sitting, very innocently looking over the hotel scrap-book and the album containing views of the neighborhood. No sooner had the old man entered than the young lady—who now showed herself to be quite as young as described, and remarkably prepossessing as to features—perceptibly turned i^ale. When the nephew entered, she turned still paler, as if she were going to faint. The young man described as an opera-singer rose with grim civility, and placed chairs for his visitors.

"Caught you, thank God !" said the old gentleman, breathlessly.

"Yes, worse luck, my lord!" murmured Signor Smithozzi, in native London English, that distinguished alien having, in fact, first seen the light in the vicinity of the City Road. " She would have been mine to-morrow. And I think that, under the peculiar circumstances, it would be wiser—considering how soon the breath of scandal will tarnish a lady's fame—to let her be mine to-morrow, just the same."

"Never!" said the old man. "Here is a lady under age, without experience, child-like in her maiden innocence and virtue, whom you have plied by your vile arts, till this morning at dawn—"

" Lord Quantock, were I not bound to respect your gray hairs—"

" Till this morning at dawn you tempted her away from her father's roof. AVliat blame can attach to her conduct that will not, on a full ex-
planation of the matter, be readily passed over in her and thrown entirely on you ? Laura, you return at once with me. I should not have arrived, after all, early enough to deliver you, if it had not been for the disinterestedness of your cousin, Captain Northbrook, who, on my discovering your flight this morning, offered—with a promptitude for which I can never sufficiently thank him—to accompany me on my journey, as the only male relative I have near me. Come, do you hear ? Put on your things; we are off at once."

" I don't want to go!" pouted the young lady.

"I dare say you don't," replied her father, dryly. " But children never know what's best for them. So, come along, and trust to my opinion."

Laura was silent and did not move, the opera gentleman looking helplessly into the fire, and the lady's cousin sitting meditatively calm, as the single one of the four whose position enabled him to survey the whole escapade with the cool criticism of a comparative outsider.

" I say to you, Laura, as the father of a daughter under age, that you instantly come with me. What ? Would you compel me to use physical force to reclaim you ?"

" I don't want to return !" again declared Laura.

" It is your duty to return, nevertheless, and at once, I inform you."

"I don't want to!"

" Now, dear Laura, this is what I say : return with me and your cousin James quietly, like a
good and repentant girl, and nothing will be said. Nobody knows what has happened as yet, and if we start at once we shall be home before it is liglit to-morrow morning. Come."

" I am not obliged to come at your bidding, father, and I would rather not!"

Now James, the cousin, during this dialogue might have been observed to grow somewhat restless and even impatient. More than once he had parted his lips to speak, but second thoughts each time held him back. The moment had come, however, when he could keep silence no longer.

" Come, madam!" he spoke out, " this farce with your father has, in my opinion, gone on long enough. Just make no more ado, and step downstairs with us."

She gave herself an intractable little twist, and did not reply.

"By the Lord Harry, Laura, I won't stand this!" he said, angrily. " Come, get on your things before I come and compel you. There is a kind of compulsion to which this talk is child's play. Come, madam—instantly, I say !"

The old nobleman turned to his nephew and said, mildly : " Leave me to insist, James. It doesn't become you. I can speak to her sharply enough, if I choose."

James, however, did not heed his uncle, and went on to the troublesome young woman : " You say)^ou don't want to come, indeed! A pretty story to tell me, that! Come, march out of the room at once, and leave that hulking fellow for me to deal with afterwards. Get on quickly— come!" and he advanced towards her, as if to pull her by the hand.

"Nay, nay," expostulated Laura's father, much surprised at his nephew's sudden demeanor. " You take too much upon yourself. Leave her to me."

"I won't leave her to you any longer!"

" You have no right, James, to address either me or her in this way ; so just hold your tongue. Come, my dear."

" I have every right!" insisted James.

" How do you make that out ?"

" I have the right of a husband."

"Whose husband?"

" Hers."

"What?"

" She's my wife."

"James!"

" Well, to cut a long story short, I may say that she secretly married me, in spite of your lordship's prohibition, about three months ago. And I must add that, though she cooled down rather quickly, everything went on smoothly enough between us for some time, in spite of the awkwardness of meeting only by stealth. We were only waiting for a convenient moment to break the news to you when this idle Adonis turned up, and after poisoning her mind against me, brought her into this disgrace."

Here the operatic luminary, who had sat in rather
an abstracted and nerveless attitude till the cousin made his declaration, fired up and cried : " I declare before Heaven that till this moment I never knew she was a wife! I found her in her father's house an unhappy girl—unhappy, as I believe, because of the loneliness and dreariness of tliat establishment, and the want of society, and for nothing else whatever. What this statement about her being your wife means I am quite at a loss to understand. Are you indeed married to him, Laura? "

Laura nodded from within her tearful handkerchief. " It was because of my anomalous position in being privately married to liira," she sobbed, " that I was unhappy at home—and—and I didn't like him so well as I did at first—and I wished I could get out of the mess I was in ! And then I saw you a few times, and when you said, ' We'll run off,' I thought I saw a way out of it all, and then I agreed to come with you-oo-ooo!"

" Well! well! well! And is this true ?" murmured the bewildered old nobleman, staring from James to Laura, and from Laura to James, as if he fancied they might be figments of the imagination. "Is this, then, James, the secret of your kindness to your old uncle in helping him to find his daughter? Good heavens ! what further depths of duplicity are there left for a man to learn !"

"I have married her, Uncle Quantock, as I said," answered James, coolly. *' The deed is done, and can't be undone by talking here."

"Where were you married?"

"At St. Mary's, Toneborough."

" When ?"

"On September 29, during the time she was visiting there."

"Who married you ?"

"I don't know. One of the curates—we were quite strangers to the place. So, instead of my assisting you to recover her, you may as well assist me."

" Never! never!" said Lord Quantock. " Madam, and sir, I beg to tell you that I wash my hands of the whole affair ! If you are man and wife, as it seems you are, get reconciled as best you may. I have no more to say or do with either of you. I leave you, Laura, in the hands of your husband, and much joy may you bring him ; though the situation, T own, is not encouraging."

Saying this, the indignant speaker pushed back his chair against the table with such force that the candlesticks rocked on their bases, and left the room,

Laura's wet eyes roved from one of the young men to the other, who now stood glaring face to face, and, being much frightened at their aspect, slipped out of the room after her father. Him, however, she could hear going out of the front door, and, not knowing where to take shelter, she crept into the darkness of an adjoining bedroom, and there awaited events with a palpitating heart.

Meanwhile the two men remaining in the sitting-room drew nearer to each other, and the opera-singer broke the silence by saying, "How could you insult me in the way you did, calling me a fellow, and accusing me of poisoning her mind towards you, when you knew very well I was as ignorant of your relation to her as an unborn babe ?"

"Oh yes, you were quite ignorant; I can believe that readily," sneered Laura's husband.

" I here call Heaven to witness that I never knew!"

^^Mecitativo —the rhythm excellent, and the tone well sustained. Is it likely that any man could win the confidence of a young fool her age, and not get that out of her? Preposterous! Tell it to the most improved new pit-stalls."

" Captain Northbrook, your insinuations are as despicable as yotir wretched person !" cried the barytone, losing all patience. And springing forward he slapped the captain in the face with the palm of his hand.

Northbrook flinched but slightly, and calmly using his handkerchief to learn if his nose was bleeding, said, "I quite expected this insult, so I came prepared." And he drew forth from a black valise which he carried in his band a small case of pistols.

The barytone started at the unexpected sight, but, recovering from his surprise, said, "Very well, as you will," though perhaps his tone showed a slight want of confidence.

" Now," continued the husband, quite confid-

ingly, "we want no parade, no nonsense, you know. Therefore we'll dispense with seconds ?"

The signor slightly nodded.

" Do you know this part of the country well ?" Cousin James went on, in the same cool and still manner. "If you don't, I do. Quite at the bottom of the rocks out there, just beyond the stream which falls over them to the shore, is a smooth sandy space, not so much shut in as to be out of the moonlight; and the way down to it from this side is over steps cut in the cliff; and we can find our way down without trouble. We—we two—will find our way down ; but only one of us will find his way up—you understand ?"

" Quite."

" Then suppose we start; the sooner it is over the better. We can order supper before we go out—supper for two; for though we are three at present—"

" Three ?"

" Yes ; you and I and she—"

"Oh yes."

" —We shall be only two by-and-by; so that, as I say, we will order supper for two—for the lady and a gentleman. Whichever comes back alive will tap at her door, and call her in to share the repast with him—she's not off the premises. But we must not alarm her now ; and, above all things, we must not let the inn people see us go out—it would look so odd for two to go out and only one come in. Ha ha!"

"Ha! ha! exactly."

"Are you ready ?"

" Oh—quite."

" Then I'll lead the way."

He went softly to the door and down-stairs, ordering supper to be ready in an hour, as he had said ; then making a feint of returning to the room again, he beckoned to the singer, and together they slipped out of the house by a side door.

The sky was now quite clear, and the wheel-marks of the brougham which had borne away Laura's father. Lord Quantock, remained distinctly visible. Soon the verge of the down was reached, the captain leading the way, and the barytone following silently, casting furtive glances at his companion and beyond him at the scene ahead. In due course they arrived at the chasm in the cliff which formed the water-fall. The outlook here was wild and picturesque in the extr'^me, and fully justified the many praises, paintings, and photographic views to which the spot had given birth. What in summer was charmingly green and gray, was now rendered weird and fantastic by the snow.

From their feet the cascade plunged downward almost vertically to a depth of eighty or a hundred feet before finally losing itself in the sand, and though the stream was but small, its impact upon jutting rocks in its descent divided it into a

hundred spirts and splashes that sent a mist into the upper air, A few marginal drippings had been frozen into icicles, but the centre flowed on unimpeded.

The operatic artist looked down as he halted, but his thoughts were plainly not of the beauty of the scene. His companion with the pistols was immediately in front of him, and there was no hand-rail on the side of the path towards the chasm. Obeying a quick impulse, he stretched out his arm, and with a superhuman thrust sent Laura's husband reeling over. A whirling human shape, diminishing downward in the moon's raj'^s farther and farther towards invisibility, a smack, smack upon the projecting ledges of rock—at first louder and heavier than that of the brook, and then scarcely to be distinguished from it—then a cessation, then the splashing of the stream as before, and the accompanying murmur of the sea, were all the incidents that disturbed the customary flow of the little water-fall.

The singer waited in a fixed attitude for a few minutes, then turning, he rapidly retraced his steps over the intervening upland towards the road, and in less than a quarter of an hour was at ^the door of the hotel. Slipping quietly in as the clock struck ten, he said to the landlord, over the bar hatchway :

" The bill as soon as you can let me have it, including charges for the supper that was ordered, though we cannot stay to eat it, I am sorry to say." He added, with forced gayety, " The lady's father and cousin have thought better of intercepting the marriage, and after quarrelling with each other have gone home independently."

"Well done, sir!" said the landlord, who still sided with this customer in preference to those who had given trouble and barely paid for baiting the horses. "' Love will find out the way!' as the saying is. Wish you joy, sir !"

Siguor Smithozzi went up-stairs, and on entering the sitting-room found that Laura had crept out from the dark adjoining chamber in his absence. She looked up at him with eyes red from weeping, and with symptoms of alarm.

"What is it?—where is he?" she said, appre-heusiveh'.

"Captain Northbrook has gone back. He says he will have no more to do with you."

"And I am quite abandoned by them!—and they'll forget me, and nobody care about me any morifi!" She began to cry afresh.

"But it is the luckiest thing that could have happened. All is just as it was before they came disturbing us. But, Laura, you ought to have told me about that private marriage, though it is all the same now; it will be dissolved, of course. You are a wid—virtually a widow."

"It is no use to reproach me for what is past. What am I to do now?"

"We go at once to Cliff-Martin. The horse has rested thoroughly these last three hours, and ho

will have no difficulty in doing an additional half-dozen miles. We shall be there before twelve, and there are late taverns in the place, no doubt. There we'll sell both horse and carriage to-morrow morning, and go by the coach to Downstaple. Once in the train we are safe."

"I agree to anything," she said, listlessly.

In about ten minutes the horse was put in, the bill paid, the lady's dried wraps put round her, and the journey resumed.

When about a mile on their way, they saw a glimmering light in advance of them. "I wonder what that is?" said the barytone, whose manner had latterly become nervous, every sound and sight causing him to turn his head.

"It is only a turnpike," said she. "That light is the lamp kept burning over the door."

"Of course, of course, dearest. How stupid I am!"

On reaching the gate they perceived that a man on foot had approached it, apparently by some more direct path than the roadway they pursued, and was, at the moment they drew up, standing in conversation with the gate-keeper.

"It is quite impossible that he could fall over the cliff by accident or the will of God on such a light night as this," the pedestrian was saying. "These two children I tell you of saw two men go along the path towards the water-fall, and ten minutes later only one of 'em came back, walking fast, like a man who wanted to get out of the way

because he had done something queer. There is no manner of doubt that he pushed the other man over, and, mark me, it will soon cause a hue-and-cry for that man."

The candle shone in the face of the signer and showed that there had arisen upon it a film of ghastliness. Laura, glancing towards him for a few moments, observed it, till, the gate-keeper having mechanically swung open the gate, her companion drove through, and they were soon again enveloped in the white silence.

Her conductor had said to Laura, just before, that he meant to inquire the way at this turnpike; but he had certainly not done so.

As soon as they had gone a little farther the omission, intentional or not, began to cause them some trouble. Beyond the secluded district which they now traversed ran the more frequented road, where progress would be easy, the snow being probably already beaten there to some extent by traffic; but they had not yet reached it, and, having no one to guide them, their journey began to appear less feasible than it had done before starting. When the little lane which ,they had entered ascended another hill, and seemed to wind round in a direction contrary to the expected route to Cliff-Martin, the question grew serious. Ever since overhearing the conversation at the turnpike, Laura had maintained a perfect silence, and had even shrunk somewhat away from the side of her lover.

"Why don't you talk, Laura," he said, with forced buoyancy, "and suggest the way we should go?"

"Oh yes, I will," she responded, a curious fear-fulness being audible in her voice.

After this she uttered a few occasional sentences which seemed to persuade him that she suspected nothing. At last he drew rein, and the weary horse stood still.

"We are in a fix," he said.

She answered, eagerly: "I'll hold the reins while you run forward to the top of the ridge, and see if the road takes a favorable turn beyond. It would give the horse a few minutes' rest, and if you find out no change in the direction, we will retrace this lane, and take the other turning."

The expedient seemed a good one in the circumstances, especially when recommended by the singular eagerness of her voice ; and placing the reins in her hands—a quite unnecessary precaution, considering the state of their hack — he stepped out and went forward through the snow till she could see no more of him.

No sooner was he gone than Laura, with a rapidity which contrasted strangely with her previous stillness, made fast the reins to the corner of the phaeton, and, slipping out on the opposite side, ran back with all her might down the hill, till, coming to an opening in the fence, she scrambled through it, and plunged into the copse which bordered this portion of the lane. Here she stood

in hiding under one of the large bushes, clinging BO closely to its umbrage as to seem but a portion of its mass, and listening intently for the faintest sound of pursuit. But nothing disturbed the stillness save the occasional slip\'7d)ing of gathered snow from the boughs, or the rustle of some wild animal over the crisp, flake-bespattered herbage. At length, apparently convinced that her former companion was either unable to find her, or not anxious to do so, in the present strange state of affairs, she crept out from the bushes, and in less than an hour found herself again approaching the door of the Prospect Hotel.

As she drew near, Laura could see that, far from being wrapped in darkness, as she might have expected, there were ample signs that all the tenants were on the alert, lights moving about the open space in front. Satisfaction was expressed in her face when she discerned that no reappearance of her barytone and his pony-carriage was causing this sensation; but it speedily gave way to grief and dismay when she saw by the lights the form of a man borne on a stretcher by two others into the porch of the hotel.

"I have caused all this," she murmured, between her quivering lips. "He has murdered him !" Running forward to the door, she hastily asked of the first person she met if the man on the stretcher was dead.

"No, miss," said the laborer addressed, eying her up and down as an unexpected apparition.

"He is still alive, they say, but not sensible. He either fell or was pushed over the water-fall; 'tis thoughted he was pushed. He is the gentleman who came here just now with the old lord, and went out afterward (as is thoughted) with a stranger who had come a little earlier. Anyhow, that's as I had it."

Laura entered the house, and acknowledging without the least reserve that she was the injured man's wife, had soon installed herself as head-nurse by the bed on which he lay. When the two surgeons who had been sent for arrived, she learned from them that his wounds were so severe as to leave but a slender hope of recovery, it being little short of miraculous that he was not killed on the spot, which his enemy had evidently reckoned to be the case. She knew who that enemy was, and shuddered.

Laura watched all night, but her husband knew nothing of her presence. During the next day he slightly recognized hei', and in the evening was able to speak. He informed the surgeons that, as was surmised, he had been pushed over the cascade by Signor Smithozzi ; but he communicated nothing to her who nursed him, not even replying to her remarks; he nodded courteously at any act of attention she rendered, and that was all.

In a day or two it was declared that everything favored his recovery, notwithstanding the severity of his injuries. Full search was made for Smithozzi, but as yet there was no intelligence of his

whereabouts, though the repentant Laura communicated all she knew. As far as could be judged, he had come back to the carriage after searching out the way, and finding the young lady missing, had looked about for her till he was tired ; then had driven on to Cliff-Martin, sold the horse and carriage next morning, and disappeared, probably by one of the departing coaches which ran thence to the nearest station, the only difference from his original programme being that he had gone alone.

During the days and weeks of that long and tedious recovery, Laura watched bj' her husband's bedside with a zeal and assiduity which would have considerably extenuated any fault save one of such magnitude as hers. That her husband did not forgive her was soon obvious. Nothing that she could do in the way of smoothing pillows, casing his position, shifting bandages, or administering draughts, could win from him more than a few measured words of thankfulness, such as he would probably have uttered to any other woman on earth Avho had performed these particular services for him.

"Dear, dear James," she said, one day, bending her face upon the bed in an excess of emotion. " How you have suffered ! It has been too cruel. I am more glad you are getting better than I can say. I have prayed for it — and I am sorry for what I have done ; T am innocent of the worst,

and—I hope you will not think me so very bad, James!"

" Oh no. On the contrary, I shall think you very good—as a nurse," he answered, the caustic severity of his tone being apparent through its weakness.

Laura let fall two or three silent tears, and said no more that day.

Somehow or other Signor Smithozzi seemed to be making good his escape. It transpired that he had not taken a passage in either of the suspected coaches, though he had certainly got out of the county; altogether, the chance of finding him was problematical.

Not only did Captain Northbrook survive his injuries, but it soon appeared that in the course of a few weeks he would find himself little if any the worse for the catastrophe. It could also be seen that Laura, while secretly hoping for her husband's forgiveness for a piece of folly of which she saw the enormity more clearly every day, was in great doubt as to what her future relations with him would be. Moreover, to add to the complication, while she, as a runaway wife, was un-forgiven by her husband, she and her husband, as a runaway couple, were unforgiven by her father, who had never once communicated with either of them since his departure from the inn. But her immediate anxiety was to win the pardon of her husband, who possibly might be bearing in mind, as he lay upon his couch, the familiar words of

Brabantio, " She has deceived her father, and may thee."

Matters went on thus till Captain Northbrook was able to walk about. He then removed with his wife to quiet apartments on the south coast, and here his recovery was rapid. Walking up the cliffs one day, supporting him by her arm as usual, she said to him, simply, "James, if I go on as I am going now, and always attend to your smallest want, and never think of anything but devotion to you, will you—try to like me a little?"

"It is a thing I must carefully consider," he said, with the same gloomy dryness that characterized all his words to her now. "When I have considered, I will tell you."

He did not tell her that evening, though she lingered long at her routine work of making his bedroom comfortable, putting the light so that it would not shine into his eyes, seeing him fall asleep, and then retiring noiselessly to her own chamber. When they met in the morning at breakfast, and she had asked him as usual how he had passed the night, she added timidly, in the silence which followed his rej^ly, "Have you considered?"

"No, I have not considered sufficiently to give you an answer."

Laura sighed, but to no purpose; and the day wore on with intense heaviness to her, and the customary modicum of strength gained to him.

The next morning she put the same question,

and looked up despairingly in his face, as though her whole life hung upon his reply.

"Yes, I have considered," he said.

«Ah!"

"We must part."

"Oh, James!"

"I cannot forgive you; no man would. Enough is settled upon you to keep you in comfort, whatever your father may do. I shall sell out, and disappear from this hemisphere."

"You have absolutely decided?" she asked, miserably. "I have nobody now to c-c-care for—"

"I have absolutely decided," he shortly returned. "We had better part here. You will go back to your father. There is no reason why I should accompany you, since my presence would only stand in the way of the forgiveness he will probably grant you if you appear before him alone. We will say farewell to each other in three days from this time. I have calculated on being ready to go on that day."

Bowed down with trouble, she withdrew to her room, and the three days were passed by her husband in writing letters and attending to other business matters, saying hardly a word to her the while. The morning of departure came; but before the horses had been put in to take the severed twain in different directions, out of sight of each other, possibly forever, the postman arrived with the morning letters.

There was one for the captain; none for her—

there were never any for her. However, on this occasion something was enclosed for her in his, which he handed her. She read it and looked up helpless.

"My dear father—is dead!" she said. In a few moments she added, in a whisper, "I must go to the Manor to bury him. . . . Will you go with me, James?"

He musingly looked out of the window. "I suppose it is an awkward and melancholy undertaking for a woman alone," he said, coldly. "Well, well—my poor uncle!—yes, I'll go with you, and see you through the business."

So they went off together instead of asunder, as planned. It is unnecessary to record the details of the journey, or of the sad week which followed it at her father's house. Lord Quantock's scat was a fine old mansion standing in its own park, and there were plenty of opportunities for husband and wife either to avoid each other, or to get reconciled if they were so minded, which one of them was at least. Captain Northbrook was not present at the reading of the will. She came to him afterwards, and found him packing up his papers, intending to start next morning, now that he had seen her through the turmoil occasioned by her father's death.

"He has left me everything that he could !" she said to her husband. " James, will you forgive me now, and stay ?"

" I cannot stay."

" Why not ?"

" I cannot stay," he repeated.

"But why?"

" I don't like you."

He acted up to his word. When she came down-stairs the next morning she was told that he had gone.

Laura bore her double bereavement as best she could. The vast mansion in which she had hitherto lived, with all its historic contents, had gone to her father's successor in the title; but her own was no unhandsome one. Around lay the undulating park, studded with trees a dozen times her own age; beyond it, the wood; beyond the wood, the farms. All this fair and quiet scene was hers. She nevertheless remained a lonely, repentant, depressed being, who would have given the greater part of everything she possessed to insure the presence and affection of that husband whose very austerity and phlegm—qualities 'that had formerly led to the alienation between them —seemed now to be adorable features in his character.

She hojDcd and hoped again, but all to no purpose. Captain Northbrook did not alter his mind and return. He was quite a different sort of man from one who altered his mind; that she was at last despairingly forced to admit. And then she left off hoping, and settled down to a mechanical routine of existence which in some measure dulled

her grief, but at the expense of all her natural animation and the sprightly wilfulness which had once charmed those who knew her, though it was perhaps all the while a factor in the production of her unhappiness.

To say that her beauty quite departed as the years rolled on would be to overstate the truth. Time is not a merciful master, as we all know, and he was not likely to act exceptionally in the case of a woman who had mental troubles to bear in addition to the ordinary weight of years. Be this as it may, eleven other winters came and went, and Laura Northbrook remained the lonely mistress of house and lands without once hearing of her husband. Every probability seemed to favor the assumption that he had died in some foreign land; and offers for her hand were not few as the probability verged on certainty with the long lapse of time. But the idea of remarriage seemed never to have entered her head for a moment. Whether she continued to hope even now for his return could not be distinctly ascertained ; at all events, she lived a life unmodified in the slightest degree from that of the first six months of his absence.

This twelfth year of Laura's loneliness and the thirtieth of her life drew on apace, and tlie season approached that liad seen the unhappy adventure for which she so long suffered. Christmas promised to be rather wet than cold, and the trees on the outskirts of Laura's estate dripped monoto-

nously from day to day upon the turnpike-road which bordered them. On an afternoon in this week, between three and four o'clock, a hired fly might have been seen driving along the highway at this point, and on reaching the top of the hill it stopped. A gentleman of middle age alighted from the vehicle.

" You need drive no farther," he said to the coachman. " The rain seems to have nearly ceased, I'll stroll a little way, and return on foot to the inn by dinner-time."

The flyman touched his hat, turned the horse, and drove back as directed. When he was out of sight, the gentleman walked on, but he had not gone far before the rain again came down pitilessly, though of this the pedestrian took little heed, going leisurely onward till he reached Laura's park gate, which he passed through. The clouds were thick and the days were short, so that by the time he stood in front of the mansion it was dark. In addition to this his appearance, which on alighting from the carriage had been untarnished, partook now of the character of a drenched wayfarer not too well blessed with this world's goods. He halted for no more than a moment at the front entrance, and going round to the servants' quarter, as if he had a preconceived purpose in so doing, there rang the bell. When a page came to him he inquired if they would kindly allow him to dry himself by the kitchen fire.

The page retired, and, after a murmured collo'quy, returned with the cook, who informed the wet and muddy man that though it was not her custom to admit strangers, she should have no particular objection to his drying himself, the night being so damp and gloomy. Therefore the wayfarer entered and sat down by the fire.

" The owner of this house is a very rich gentleman, no doubt?" he asked, as he watched the meat turning on the spit.

" 'Tis not a gentleman, but a lady," said the cook.

"A widow, I presume?"

"A sort of widow. Poor soul, her husband is gone abroad, and has never been heard of for many years."

" She sees plenty of company, no doubt, to make up for his absence?"

" No, indeed—hardly a soul. Service here is as bad as being in a nunnery."

In short, the wayfarer, who had at first been so coldly received, contrived by his frank and engaging manner to draw the ladies of the kitchen into a most confidential conversation, in which Laura's history was minutely detailed, from the day of her husband's departure to the present. The salient feature in all their discourse was her unflagging devotion to his memory.

Having apparently learned all that he wanted to know—among other things that she was at this moment, as always, alone—the traveller said he was quite dry; and thanking the servants for their kindness, departed as he had come. On emerging into the darkness he did not, however, go down the avenue by which he had arrived. He simply walked round to the front door. There he rang, and the door was opened to him by a man-servant whom he had not seen during his sojourn at the other end of the house.

In answer to the servant's inquiry for his name, he said, ceremoniously, " Will you tell The Honorable Mrs. Northbrook that the man she nursed many years ago, after a frightful accident, has called to thank her?"

The footman retreated, and it was rather a long time before any further signs of attention were apparent. Then he was shown into the drawing-room, and the door closed behind him.

On the couch was Laura, trembling and pale. She parted her lips and held out her hands to him, but could not speak. But he did not require speech, and in a moment they were in each other's arms.

Strange news circulated through that mansion and the neighboring town on the next and following days. But the world has a way of getting used to things, and the intelligence of the return of The Honorable Mrs. Northbrook's long-absent husband was soon received with comparative calm.

A few days more brought Christmas, and the forlorn home of Laura Northbrook blazed from basement to attic with light and cheerfulness. Not that the house was overcrowded with visitors, but many were present, and the apathy of a dozen years came at length to an end. The animation which set in thus at the close of the old year did not diminish on the arrival of the new; and by the time its twelve months had likewise run the course of its predecessors, a son had been added to the dwindled line of the Northbrook family.

At the conclusion of this narrative the Spark was thanked, with a manner of some surprise, for nobody had credited him with a taste for tale-telling. Though it had been resolved that this story should be the last, a few of the weatherbound listeners were for sitting on into the small hours over their pipes and glasses, and raking up yet more episodes of family history. But the majority murmured reasons for soon getting to their lodgings.

It was quite dark without, except in the immediate neighborhood of the feeble street-lamps, and before a few shop-windows which had been hardily kept open in spite of the obvious unlikelihood of any chance customer traversing the muddy thoroughfares at that hour.

By one, by two, and by three the benighted members of the Field Club rose from their seats, shook hands, made appointments, and dropped away to their respective quarters, free or hired, hoping for a fair morrow. It would probably be not until the next summer meeting, months away in the future, that the easy intercourse which now existed between them all would repeat itself. The crimson maltster, for instance, knew that on the following market-day his friends the president, the rural dean, and the bookworm would pass him in the street, if they met him, with the barest nod of civility, the president and the colonel for social reasons, the bookworm for intellectual reasons, and the rural dean for moral ones, the latter being a stanch teetotaler, dead against John Barleycorn, The sentimental member knew that when, on his rambles, he met his friend the bookworm with a pocket-copy of something or other under his nose, the latter would not love his companionship as he had done to-day; and the president, the aristocrat, and the farmer knew that affairs political, sporting, domestic, or agricultural would exclude for a long time all rumination on the characters of dames gone to dust for scores of years, however beautiful and noble they may have been in their day.

The last member at length departed, the attendant at the museum lowered the fire, the curator locked up the rooms, and soon there was only a single pirouetting flame on the top of a single coal to make the bones of the icthyosaurus seem to leap, the stuffed birds to wink, and to draw a smile from the varnished skulls of Vespasian's Soldiery.

THE END

Printed in Great Britain
by Amazon